D0108835

Hospital
of the
Transfiguration

Hospital
of the
Transfiguration

Stanislaw Lem

Translated from the Polish
by William Brand

A Helen and Kurt Wolff Book
Harcourt Brace Jovanovich, Publishers
San Diego   New York   London

Falmouth Public Library
Falmouth, Mass. 02540

Copyright © 1982 by Stanislaw Lem
English translation copyright © 1988
by Harcourt Brace Jovanovich, Inc.

All rights reserved. No part of this publication may be reproduced
or transmitted in any form or by any means, electronic or mechanical,
including photocopy, recording, or any information storage and re-
trieval system, without permission in writing from the publisher.

Requests for permission to make copies of any part of the work should
be mailed to: Permissions, Harcourt Brace Jovanovich, Publishers,
Orlando, Florida 32887.

Library of Congress Cataloging-in-Publication Data
Lem, Stanisław.
[Szpital przemienienia. English]
Hospital of the Transfiguration/Stanislaw Lem; translated
from the Polish by William Brand.—1st ed.
p. cm.
Translation of: Szpital przemienienia.
"A Helen and Kurt Wolff Book."
ISBN 0-15-142186-2
I. Title.
PG7158.L39S913 1988
891.8'537—dc19   87-33659

Designed by Beth Tondreau Design

Printed in the United States of America

First edition

A B C D E

TO MY FATHER

Contents

Hospital
of the
Transfiguration

A Country Funeral

The train stopped briefly in Nieczawy. Stefan had barely pushed through the crowd to the doors and jumped off when the locomotive wheezed and the wheels began to drum behind him. For an hour he had been worrying that he would miss his stop; that problem had overshadowed all others, even the goal of the journey itself. Now, breathing the sharp outdoor air after the stuffiness of the train, he walked uncertainly, squinting in the sun, at once liberated and helpless, as if he had been jolted out of a deep sleep.

It was one of the last days of February and the sky was streaked with light clouds pale at their edges. The snow had been partly melted by the thaw and sat heavily in the hollows and gorges, exposing clumps of brush and bushes, blackening the road with mud and baring the clay hillsides. Chaos, harbinger of change, had appeared in a landscape once uniformly white.

This thought cost Stefan a careless step and water seeped into his shoe. He shuddered with disgust. The snorting of the locomotive was fading behind the Bierzyniec hills; Stefan could hear what sounded like an elusive chirping of crickets that seemed to come from all over: the unvarying sound of melting. In his woolly raglan, soft felt hat, and low city shoes, he knew that he cut an incongruous figure against the background of rolling hills. Dazzling streams danced and flashed along the road up to the village. Hopping from stone to stone, he finally made it to the crossroads and glanced at his watch. It was almost one. No specific time had been set for the funeral, but he felt he ought to hurry. The body had left Kielce in its coffin yesterday. So it should already be at the church, since the telegram had contained that vague mention of a Mass. Or was it exequies? He couldn't remember, and it annoyed him to be pondering a liturgical question. It was a ten-minute walk to his uncle's house, and just as far to the cemetery, but what if the procession went the long way to stop at the church? Stefan moved toward the bend in the road, stopped, took a few steps back, and stopped again. He saw an old peasant coming along a path between the fields, shouldering the kind of cross usually carried at the head of a funeral procession. Stefan wanted to call out to him, but didn't dare. Clenching his teeth, he strode toward the cemetery. The peasant reached the cemetery wall and disappeared. Stefan could not tell whether he had gone on toward the village; in desperation he gathered up the folds of his coat like an old woman and charged through the puddles. The road to the cemetery skirted a small hill overgrown with hazel. Ignoring the way his feet sank into the snow and the twigs lashed his face, Stefan ran to the top. The thicket ended abruptly. He came back down onto the road just in front of the cemetery. It was quiet and empty, with no trace of the peasant. Stefan's haste evaporated at once. He looked mournfully at his muddy trouser cuffs and, gasping for breath, peered over the gate. There was no one in the cemetery. When he pushed it open, the gate's dreadful shriek subsided into a sad groan. Dirty, crusted snow covered the graves in billows that left mounds at the foot of the crosses, whose wooden ranks

2

ended at a wild lilac bush. Beyond stood the stone monument of the Princes of Nieczawy and the larger, separate crypt of the Trzyniecki family, black with names and dates in gold letters, three birches standing at the granite headstone. In an empty strip that separated the mausoleum from the rest of the cemetery like a no-man's-land gaped a freshly dug grave whose clay blotted the surrounding white. Stefan stopped dead, shocked. Apparently the mausoleum was full, and with no time or way to enlarge it, a Trzyniecki would have to go into the ground like anyone else. Stefan imagined how Uncle Anzelm must have felt about this, but there was no real choice: since Nieczawy had once belonged to the Trzynieckis, all the dead were buried here, and although only Uncle Ksawery's house now remained, the custom endured. At each death family representatives came to the funeral from all over Poland.

Crystal icicles hung from the arms of the crosses and the wild lilac branches, and the quietly dripping water made holes in the snow. Stefan stood for a moment before the open grave. He should have gone to the house, but he found that idea so unappealing that instead he paced between the crosses of the country cemetery. The names, burned with wire into the boards, had turned into black stains. Many had disappeared entirely, leaving smooth wood. Floundering in the snow that chilled his feet, Stefan walked around the cemetery until he stopped suddenly at a grave marked by a large birch cross with a piece of metal nailed to it. The inscription was done with flourishes:

Traveller, Tell Poland Her Sons Lie Beneath
Faithful To Her Until The Hour Of Their Death.

Below was a list of names and ranks. An unknown soldier came last. There was also a September 1939 date.

Not six months had passed since that September, but the

3

inscription would not have endured the foul weather and frost had it not been retouched by some evocative hand. A similar care showed in the fir branches that covered the grave, which was so small that it was hard to believe that several people were buried in it. Stefan lingered a moment, moved but also uncertain, for he was not sure whether he should take off his hat. Unable to decide, he moved on. The cold of the snow was getting to him; he kicked his shoes together and looked at his watch again. It was twenty past one. He had to hurry if he wanted to get to the house in time, but it occurred to him that he could simplify his ceremonial participation in this funeral by waiting for the procession at the cemetery, so he turned back and stood again at the excavation that would receive Uncle Leszek's body.

Looking into the hole, Stefan realized how deep it was. He knew enough of the gravedigger's mysterious technique to understand that the grave had purposely been dug deep enough to contain a future coffin—that of Aunt Aniela, Leszek's widow. The realization made him feel like an inadvertent witness to some impropriety; he forced himself to pull away and found himself looking down rows of lopsided crosses. His mind had been sensitized by loneliness, and the thought that differences in living standards persisted even among the dead struck him as absurd and pitiful. He breathed deeply for a moment. It was absolutely quiet. Not the slightest sound came from the nearby village, and even the crows, whose cawing had accompanied him as he walked, had fallen silent. The foreshortened shadows of the crosses lay on the snow and the chill rose from his feet up through his body to his heart. He crouched, burying his hands in his pockets, and in the right one found a small bundle—bread his mother had tucked there before he left home. Suddenly hungry, he took out the bread and unwrapped the thin paper. Ham shined pink between the

4

slices. He brought the bread to his mouth but could not bring himself to eat standing at the freshly dug grave. He told himself this was going too far—what was it, really, but a hole dug in clay?—but he could not help it. A piece of bread in his hand, he waded through the snow toward the cemetery gate. As he passed the nameless crosses he searched in vain for some individual trait, some evidence of the dead, in their ungainly forms. He thought that efforts to maintain graves expressed a belief that reached back to times immemorial. Regardless of the precepts of religion, in spite of the obvious fact of decay, and contrary to the evidence of their senses, people still acted as though the dead led some sort of existence deep in the earth—uncomfortable perhaps, maybe even dreadful, but an existence just the same, one that lasted as long as some identifying mark on the surface remained.

He reached the gate, looked once more at the distant rows of crosses sunk in the snow and at the yellowish stain of the open grave, then walked out onto the muddy road. As he mulled over his last thoughts again, the absurdity of funeral rites struck him as obvious and his own participation in the day's ceremony seemed embarrassing. For a moment he was even angry at his parents for persuading him to come all this way, but that was stranger still, since he was representing not himself, but his father, who was ill.

He ate the bread and ham slowly, moistening each mouthful with his saliva and swallowing with some effort, for his throat was dry. His mind kept working. Yes, he thought, the people who paid the least heed to the arguments of this world believed somewhere within themselves in the "continued existence of the dead." If concern for the grave were a mere expression of love and sorrow for the departed, then taking care of the visible, above-ground part of the grave would suffice. But if that were the only motive of human funeral ceremonies, it

5

could not account for the pains taken over the appearance of the corpse, the dressing of the deceased, the pillow placed under the head, the box as resistant as possible to the forces of nature. No, such actions betrayed a dark and uncomprehending faith that the dead endured, a faith in that gruesome, horrifying living existence in the narrow confines of the coffin, apparently preferable, in people's instinctive opinion, to complete annihilation and union with the earth.

Not knowing the answer himself, he began walking toward the village and the church spire that glistened in the sunlight. Suddenly he glimpsed some movement at the bend in the road and quickly shoved the bread back into his pocket before he realized what he was doing.

The dark blot of the procession appeared around the little hill, where the road curved and ran below a steep clay wall. The people were too far away for him to make out their faces. He could see only the cross swaying at the head, the white spots of the priests' surplices just behind it, the roof of a truck, and in the background tiny figures moving so slowly that they seemed to be marching in place, rocking with a certain majesty, the motion made almost grotesque by the diminishing effects of distance. It was hard to take this miniature funeral seriously and wait for it with the proper gravity, but it was no easier to go forward to meet it. It looked like a randomly scattered collection of dolls bouncing at the foot of a great clay landslide, from which the wind carried snatches of incomprehensible lamentations. Stefan wanted to get there as quickly as possible, but he dared not move. Instead, taking off his hat, he stood motionless at the edge of the road, the wind now blowing his hair into disarray. An onlooker would have been hard put to tell whether he was a belated participant in the solemnities or just a chance passerby. The walking figures grew in size as they came nearer, and imperceptibly got close enough to erase

6

the peculiar effect the distance had had on Stefan. Now, finally, he was able to make out the old peasant leading the way with the cross, the two priests, the truck from the nearby sawmill inching along behind them, and finally all the scattered members of his family. The discordant singing of the village women droned on endlessly; when the procession was a few dozen paces away, Stefan heard a ringing, first a few uneven sounds, and then a full, strong tolling that echoed with dignity throughout the countryside. When the bell sounded, Stefan thought that the Szymczaks' little Wicek must have been pulling the cord, only to be supplanted by the more proficient, redheaded Tomek, but he suddenly remembered that "little" Wicek would be a man of his own age by now, and that nothing had been heard of Tomek since his departure for the city. But the battle over the right to ring the bell apparently persisted among the younger generation of Nieczawy.

Life entails situations unforeseen by handbooks of etiquette, situations so difficult and delicate that they require great tact and self-confidence. Lacking these virtues, Stefan had no idea how to go about joining the procession; he stood indecisively with a distinct feeling that he was being watched, which only compounded his confusion. Fortunately, the cortège halted just before the church. One of the priests walked over to the truck and asked the driver a question; the driver nodded, and some peasants Stefan didn't know climbed out of the truck and began to remove the coffin. There was some confusion during which Stefan managed to slip into the group standing around the truck. He had just noticed the thickset, short-necked figure and graying head of Uncle Ksawery, who was supporting Aunt Aniela, dressed all in black, when a muffled call went out that more people were needed to carry the coffin into the church. Stefan stepped forward, but as always when everyone was watching and some ever so slightly responsible action was required, he made a mess of it and his eagerness produced no more than a nervous stumble in the truck's direction. In the end the coffin was lifted over the heads of those assembled without his help, and he was left to carry the fur coat that Uncle Anzelm, his father's oldest brother, had taken off and handed to him at the last moment.

Stefan carried the coat into the church. He was among the last to enter but was deeply convinced that by carrying the enormous bearskin he too was contributing to the ceremony. The bell stuttered to the end of its monotonous song, both priests disappeared for a moment and emerged again when the family had settled into the pews, and the first words of the Latin exequy were pronounced from the altar.

Stefan could have sat down, since there were plenty of seats and his uncle's fur coat was not exactly light, but he preferred to stand in the depths of the nave bearing his burden which, perhaps just because it was so heavy, seemed to atone for his earlier awkwardness. The coffin lay at the altar and Uncle Anzelm, after lighting the candles around it, walked straight toward Stefan, who felt slightly unnerved by this attention, for he had hoped the darkness at the foot of the pillar where he was standing would preserve his anonymity.

His uncle squeezed his shoulder and whispered under the priest's melodic voice, "Is your father ill?"

"Yes, Uncle. He had an attack yesterday."

"Those stones again?" asked Uncle Anzelm in a piercing whisper, trying to take the fur from Stefan.

But Stefan did not want to let go and mumbled, "No, please don't, I'll . . ."

"Come on, give me the fur, you fool, it's cold as hell in here," his uncle said with good humor, but too loudly. Anzelm took the fur, threw it over his shoulders, and walked to the pew where the widow sat, leaving Stefan embarrassed; the young man could feel himself turning red.

8

This incident, trivial as it was, ruined his whole stay in the church. He recovered only when he spotted Uncle Ksawery sitting at the far corner of the last pew. He took comfort in imagining how out of place Ksawery must have felt, an atheist so militant he tried to convert each new parish priest. Uncle Ksawery was an old bachelor, hot-tempered and outspoken, an enthusiastic subscriber to Boy's library of French classics, a proponent of birth control, and the only doctor in a twelve-kilometer radius to boot. The Kielce relatives had long tried to evict him from the old house, battling for years in the township and district courts, but Ksawery had won every round, cheating them so cunningly—as they put it—that they finally gave up. Now he sat with his big hands resting heavily on the rail, separated from his conquered relatives by a pew.

The organ's deep voice sounded, and Stefan shuddered as he recalled the humble saintliness that had fired his soul as a small boy; he had always held organ music in deep respect. The exequies unfolded properly. One of the priests lighted incense in a small censer and circled the coffin, surrounding it with a cloud of fragrant though acrid smoke. Stefan looked for the widow. She was sitting in the second pew, bent, patient, strangely indifferent to the words of the priest who, in florid Latin, kept singing the last name of the deceased, which was also her last name, repeating it with exultation and insistence. But he was not addressing any of the living, only Providence, requesting, begging, almost commanding Its benevolence toward that which was no more.

The organ fell silent, and again it was necessary to shoulder the coffin that now rested on the catafalque before the altar, but this time Stefan did not even try to help. Everyone stood up and, clearing their throats, prepared for the way ahead. When the gently swaying coffin left the shadowed nave and reached the church steps, there was some jostling—the elongated, heavy box pitched forward threateningly, but a forest of upraised hands rebalanced it and it emerged into the afternoon sun with no more than a brisk bobbing, as if excited by the close call.

Just then a foolish and macabre thought ran through Stefan's mind: it must indeed be Uncle Leszek in there, because he had always loved practical jokes, especially on solemn occasions. Stefan quickly squelched the idea, or rather recast it in terms of healthy reason: it was absurd, that wasn't his uncle in the coffin but only the remains of his person, remains so embarrassing and troublesome that their removal from the domain of the living required the devising and staging of this whole interminable, intricate, and rather unconvincing ceremony.

He followed the coffin with the others, heading for the open cemetery gate. There were about twenty people in the procession; without the coffin they would have made a strange impression, because they wore clothes somewhere between dress appropriate for a long journey (almost all of them had traveled to Nieczawy from far away) and evening wear, predominately black. Most of the men wore high riding boots and some of the women were in high laced shoes like boots, trimmed with fur. Someone Stefan could not recognize from behind was wearing an army coat with no insignia, as if the patches had been ripped off; that coat, which held Stefan's eye for a long moment, was the only reminder of the September Campaign. No, he thought, not really—there was also the absence of people who would have been there under different circumstances, like Uncle Antoni and Cousin Piotr, both of whom were in German prison camps.

The singing—or rather wailing—of the village women was an endless repetition of "Give him eternal rest, O Lord, and everlasting light." It bothered Stefan only for a moment, then he ceased to be aware of it. The strung-out procession bunched

10

up at the cemetery gate, then followed the upraised coffin in a black line between the graves. Prayers began again over the open grave. Stefan found this a bit excessive, and thought that if he were a believer, he would wonder whether the being to whom they were addressed might not regard such endlessly renewed pleas as importunate.

Someone tugged at his sleeve before he could finish formulating this last thought. He turned and saw the wide, hawk-nosed face of Uncle Anzelm in his fur collar, who asked, again too loudly, "Have you had anything to eat today?" Without waiting for an answer, he quickly added, "Don't worry, there'll be bigos!" Anzelm slapped Stefan on the back, hunched his shoulders, and waded in among the relatives, who stood looking at the still-empty grave. He touched each of them with a finger, moving his lips as he did so. Stefan thought this quite curious until he realized that his uncle was simply counting the crowd. Then Anzelm whispered loudly to a village boy, who backed away from the black circle in rustic reverence, walked to the gate, and then broke into a run toward Ksawery's house.

Having completed these host's duties, Uncle Anzelm returned, whether by accident or design, to Stefan's side and even found the time to point out how colorful the group around the grave was. Four stout boys then placed the coffin on cords and lowered it into the yawning hole, where it landed askew. One of the boys, holding onto the edge with dirty hands, climbed down and shoved it hard with his boot. Stefan was hurt by this rough treatment of an object that had so far been accorded uninterrupted respect. In this he found further confirmation of his thesis that the living, no matter how they tried to polish the rough edges of the passage out of life, could find no consistent and harmonious attitude to the dead.

The particular wartime aspect of the funeral was evident

after the men with shovels, working with an almost feverish energy, closed the grave and formed the elongated mound of earth above it. Under normal circumstances, it would have been unthinkable for the mourners to leave the cemetery without strewing their relative's grave with flowers, but flowers were out of the question in this first winter after the invasion. Even the greenhouses on the nearby Przetułowicz estate, where all the glass had been broken during the battle, left the Trzynieckis down, so only spruce boughs were laid on the grave. The prayers finished, their respects paid, the mourners turned from the green mound and made their way, one by one, down the snowy path to the muddy, puddle-strewn road back to the village.

When the priests, who were as cold as everyone else, removed their white surplices, things seemed more normal. Other changes, less explicit, came over the rest of the mourners. Their solemnity, a sort of slowing of movement and glance, fell away. A naive observer might have thought that they had been walking on tiptoe and had now got tired of it.

On the way back Stefan made sure to stay away from Aunt Aniela, not out of lack of affection or sympathy but because he was well aware of what a loving wife she had been to his uncle, and no matter how hard he tried, he would have been unable to utter a single phrase of condolence. In the meantime, panic spread over the mourners' faces when they saw Uncle Ksawery take Aunt Melania Skoczyńska by the arm. Stefan was dumbfounded at the strange and rare sight. Ksawery hated Aunt Melania, had called her an old bottle of poison and said that the ground she walked on ought to be disinfected. Aunt Melania, an old spinster, had long devoted herself to stirring up family quarrels in which she could maintain a sweet neutrality while going from house to house spreading venomous remarks and rumors that fostered bitterness and did great

12

damage, since the Trzynieckis were all stubborn once their emotions were aroused.

When he saw Stefan, Ksawery called from a distance, "Welcome, my brother in Aesculapius! Have you got your diploma yet?!"

Naturally Stefan had to stop to greet them, and after he quickly touched his maiden aunt's frigid hand with his nose, the three walked together toward the house, now just visible through the trees. It was yellow as egg yolk, the very essence of a manor house, with classic columns and a large veranda overlooking the orchard. They stopped at the entrance to wait for the others. Uncle Ksawery revealed an unexpected flair for acting the host, expansively inviting everyone inside as though he feared they would drift off into the snowy, marshy countryside.

At the door, Stefan suffered a brief but intense torment, as an avalanche of greetings suspended during the funeral descended on him. During the kissing of hands and pecking of cheeks he had to be careful not to confuse the men with the women, which he may have done, he was not quite sure. Finally, amid the wiping of boots and waving sleeves of shed coats, he entered the drawing room. The sight of the enormous grandfather clock with its inlaid pendulum made him feel instantly at home, because whenever he visited Nieczawy he slept under the deer-head trophy on the wall opposite. In the corner stood the battered armchair in whose hairy depths he rested during the day and in which he was sometimes awakened at night by the loud striking of the clock, its unearthly face shining round and cold in the moonlight, glowing in stillness like the moon itself. But the traffic in the room prevented him from wallowing in childhood memories. The ladies sat in armchairs, the gentlemen stood enveloped in clouds of cigarette smoke. The conversation had barely begun when the

13

double doors of the dining room opened to reveal Anzelm standing on the threshold. Frowning like a benevolent, somewhat absent-minded emperor, he invited everyone to table. A proper funeral dinner was out of the question, of course—the very term would have rung resoundingly false—and the weary, sorrowful relatives were instead invited to a modest snack.

The guests included one of the priests who had led the procession to the cemetery, thin, sallow, and tired, but smiling as though happy that everything had gone so well. The priest, bending stiffly low, was talking to Great-aunt Jadwiga, the matriarch of the Trzynieckis, a small woman in a dress that was too big for her. She seemed to have withered and shrunk so much inside the garment that she had to hold her hands up as if in prayer to keep the sleeves from falling over her dry fingers. The distracted, contrary expression on her small, slightly flat, and childish face made it seem as though she were contemplating some senile, childish prank instead of listening to the priest. She looked up with her round blue eyes and, spotting Stefan, called him over with a finger bent into a hook. Stefan swallowed manfully and approached his great-aunt. She looked up at Stefan carefully and somewhat slyly before saying in a surprisingly deep voice, "Stefan, the son of Stefan and Michalina?"

"Yes, yes," he acknowledged eagerly.

She smiled at him, pleased either by her memory or by her great-nephew's appearance; she took his hand in her own painfully sharp grip, brought it close to her eyes, examined it from both sides, and then released it suddenly, as if it contained nothing of interest after all. Then she looked Stefan in the eye and said, "Do you know that your father wanted to be a saint?"

She cackled softly three times before Stefan had a chance to answer, and added for no apparent reason: "We still have his diapers somewhere. We saved them."

14

Then she looked straight ahead and said no more. In the meantime, Uncle Anzelm had reappeared and vigorously invited everyone to the dining room, bowing perfectly in Great-aunt Jadwiga's direction. He led her into the dining room first, and that drew in the others. His great-aunt had not forgotten Stefan, for she asked him to sit beside her, which he did with something like pleased despair. Sitting down at the table was a little chaotic. Then Uncle Ksawery, the host, unseen until now, came in with a huge porcelain tureen smelling of bigos. He served each of the guests in turn, his nicotine-stained doctor's fingers ladling bigos onto the plates so forcefully that the women drew back to protect their clothes. This warmed up the atmosphere. Everyone talked about the same thing: the weather, and their hope for an allied offensive in the spring.

The tall, broad-shouldered man whose military coat Stefan had noticed earlier sat at his left. He was one of Stefan's mother's relatives, a tenant farmer from Poznań named Grzegorz Niedzic. He sat in silence, and froze as if he had been touched by a wand whenever he changed position. His smile was simple, shy, and somehow innocent, as if he were apologizing for the inconvenience caused by his presence. The smile made a peculiar contrast with his sunburned, mustached face and ill-fitting clothes, unmistakably sewn from an army blanket.

It was obvious at the table that post-funeral formalities were nothing new to this assembly, and it occurred to Stefan that the last family gathering he had attended was in Kielce at Christmas. The memory was triggered because unanimity in the family was rare, usually forthcoming only after funerals, and although nobody had died last Christmas, the intensity of shared sorrow had been similar—the occasion was the burial of the fatherland.

Stefan felt uneasy in this company. He disliked large groups, especially formal ones. What's more, when he looked at the priest seated opposite him, he was sure that such a reverend presence would provoke Ksawery to blasphemy, and he had an innate aversion to scenes. He also felt bad because his father, whom he represented, did not enjoy the best of reputations here, being the only inventor in memory among a family of landowners and doctors and at that an inventor who had reached his sixties without inventing anything.

Nor was the mood lightened by the presence of Grzegorz Niedzic, apparently a born non-talker, who answered attempts at conversation by smiling warmly and peering sympathetically into his plate. And Stefan became especially eager to get a conversation going when he noticed that Ksawery's eyes were sparkling darkly, a sure sign that trouble was brewing. And so it was. In a moment of relative silence broken only by the ringing of cutlery, Ksawery said to Stefan, "You must have felt as out of place as a eunuch in a harem in that church, eh?"

The crack was indirectly aimed at the priest, and Ksawery doubtless had a sharp rejoinder ready, but he had no chance to use it, because the relatives, as if on command, began speaking loudly and fast. Everyone knew that Ksawery was wont to do such things, and the sole remedy was to drown him out. Then one of the village women called Ksawery into the kitchen to look for the cold pork, and the meal was interrupted.

Stefan amused himself by looking at the collection of family faces. First prize unquestionably went to Uncle Anzelm. Well-built, stocky, massive rather than fat, Anzelm had a face that no one would call handsome, but it was perfectly lordly and he wore it beautifully. That face, along with the bearskin coat, seemed to be the sole remnant of the great manorial possessions he had lost twenty years earlier, supposedly consequent to the indulgence of a variety of passions, although Stefan did not know for sure. What he did know was that Anzelm was dy-

16

namic, benevolent, and short-tempered, able to stay angry longer than anyone else in the family—for five, even ten years, so that not even Aunt Melania could remember the cause. No one dared try to settle these marathon quarrels, because an admission of ignorance of the original offense automatically triggered a special wrath reserved for clumsy mediators. Stefan's father had once been burned this way. But the death of a relative silenced all of Anzelm's hostility, and everyone else's too. The *treuga Dei* would reign for a few days or a couple of weeks, depending on circumstances. At such times, Ksawery's innate good nature would shine in every glance and word; he would be so inexhaustibly generous and forgiving that Stefan would believe that the rage had been not just suspended but abolished. Then the natural state of Uncle Anzelm's feelings, violated by death, would be reasserted: implacable hatred would triumph and remain unchanged for years—until the next funeral.

As a boy, Stefan had been immensely impressed by how resistant to time Uncle Anzelm and his emotions were; later, as a student, he partly understood the mechanism. His uncle's great anger had once been bolstered by the power of his possessions, in other words, by his ability to threaten family members with disinheritance, but Anzelm's unbending character had allowed his anger to outlive his financial collapse, so that he was still feared even without the threat. But this understanding had not freed Stefan from the mixture of respect and dread he felt for his father's oldest brother.

The missing cold pork turned up unexpectedly inside the black sideboard. When the enormous block of meat was removed from the depths of the ancient piece of furniture, its dark color reminded Stefan of the coffin and made him uneasy for a moment. Then, with a stamping of feet and a clatter, a spit of roast duck was carried in, along with a jar of tart cranberries and a bowl of steaming potatoes. The modest snack thus became a feast, especially since Uncle Ksawery pulled bottle after bottle of wine from the sideboard. All along, Stefan had felt distant from the others; but now his sense of estrangement grew. He had been bothered by the tone of the conversation and the skill with which the subject of death was avoided, though that, after all, was the reason they were all together. Now his indignation peaked, and everything seemed to ring false, including grief over the lost fatherland, accompanied as it was by the brisk motion of silverware and the chomping of jaws. No one seemed to remember Uncle Leszek lying underground in the empty cemetery. Stefan looked with distaste at the flushed faces of his neighbors, and his disgust spread beyond the family and became contempt for the world. For the time being he could express it only by refraining from eating, which he did so well that he left the table hungry.

But before he left, a change came over Grzegorz Niedzic, Stefan's silent neighbor to the left. For some time Grzegorz had been wiping his mustache with irritation and glancing obliquely at the door, as if measuring the distance. He was plainly preparing for something. Then suddenly he leaned toward Stefan and announced that he had to leave to catch the train to Poznań.

"What do you want to do, travel all night?" Stefan asked without thinking.

"Yes, I have to be at work tomorrow morning."

He explained that the Germans barely tolerated Poles in Poznań, and he had had a lot of trouble getting a day off. It took all night to get to Nieczawy, and he had to start back right away. Without finishing his clumsy explanation, he drew a deep breath, stood up so violently that he almost took the tablecloth with him, bowed blindly in all directions, and started for the door. There was an outcry of questions and protest, but the man, stubbornly silent, bowed again at the threshold and disappeared into the hall. Uncle Ksawery went after him, and a moment later the outside door slammed. Stefan looked out the window. It was dark. The tall figure in the skimpy overcoat loomed in his imagination, tramping the muddy road. Looking at the abandoned chair to his left, Stefan noticed that the starched fringes of the tablecloth had been carefully combed and separated, and he felt a warm rush of compassion for this unknown distant cousin who would spend two nights being jostled in dark trains to accompany a dead relative for a few hundred steps.

The table looked mournful, as after any big meal, the plates piled with picked bones coated with congealed fat. There was a moment of silence as men reached in their pockets for cigarettes, the priest wiped his glasses with a chamois cloth, and the great-aunt fell into a rapt trance that would have been a nap except that her eyes were wide open. Against this background of quiet, the widow Aniela spoke for the first time. Immobile, head down, she said into the tablecloth, "You know, it's all somehow ridiculous."

Her voice faltered. No one broke the even deeper silence that followed. This was unprecedented; nobody was prepared for it. The priest went at once to Aunt Aniela, moving with the strained competence of a doctor who feels he ought to administer first aid but is at a loss what to do. He simply stood murmuring over her, both of them black, she in her dress, he in his cassock, his face lemony, his eyelids puffy, until they were all saved by the servants—or rather by the two village women acting as servants for the occasion, who entered and began noisily clearing the table.

Uncle Ksawery conferred in hurried whispers with the relatives in the gloomy drawing room, near the shiny glass of the oak bookcase, under the inlaid, lightly smoking oil lamp with the orange shade. He insisted that some stay the night, informed others about train schedules, and gave directions about who was to be wakened and when. Stefan had planned to start for home, but when he found that there was no train until three in the morning, he let himself be persuaded to stay the night. He would sleep in the drawing room opposite the clock, so he had to wait for the others to leave. It was nearly midnight when they did. Stefan washed quickly, undressed by the light of the flickering lamp, blew out the flame, and climbed between the cold sheets with an unpleasant shudder. He had felt sleepy before, but the feeling now left him as if plucked away by an invisible hand. For a long time he lay on his back trying to fall asleep, but the clock, invisible in the darkness, seemed to strike the quarters and hours with exaggerated emphasis.

His thoughts, indefinite and vague, meandered through bits and pieces of the day's experiences, but they tended inevitably in one direction. The whole family was made of fire and stone, passion and inflexibility. The Kielce Trzynieckis were famous for their greed, Uncle Anzelm for his rage, his great-aunt for some romantic madness lost in the mists of time. This force of destiny showed differently in different people. Stefan's father was an inventor who did all other things strictly out of compulsion; he waved the world away as though it were a fly; sometimes he lost days, living Thursday twice and then realizing that Wednesday had been lost. This was not true absentmindedness, just excessive concentration on whatever idea was driving him at the moment. If he was not sleeping or ill, you could bet that he would be sitting in his tiny attic-workshop, among Bunsen burners, alcohol lamps, and glowing instruments, wreathed in the smell of acid and metal, measuring, polishing, welding. These actions that went into the process of inventing never ceased, though the planned inventions changed. His father went from one failure to the next

20

with undiminished faith and a passion so powerful that strangers thought he was obtuse or oblivious. He had never treated Stefan like a child. He spoke to the small boy who appeared in his dimly lighted workshop the way he would have talked to an adult who was hard of hearing, the conversation full of interruptions and misunderstandings. Paying them no mind, moving from lathe to jig and back again, his mouth full of screws and his smock singed, he spoke to Stefan as if he were delivering a lecture, with pauses for particularly absorbed tinkering. What did he talk about? Stefan no longer really remembered, for he had been too young to grasp the meaning of those speeches, but he thought they went something like this: "What has happened and passed no longer exists, just as if it had never been. It's like a cake you ate yesterday. Now there's nothing left. That's why you can make yourself a past you never had. If you just believe in it, it will be as if you really lived it."

Another time he said: "Did you want to be born? You didn't, did you? Well, you couldn't have wanted to, because you didn't exist. I didn't want you to be born, either. I mean, I wanted a son, but not you, because I didn't know you, so I couldn't want you. I wanted a son in general, but you're the reality."

Stefan seldom spoke and never asked his father questions, except once, when he was fifteen. He asked his father what he would do once he had finally perfected his invention. His father's face darkened, and after a long silence he replied that he would start inventing something else. "Why?" Stefan asked rashly. This question, like its predecessor, arose from a deeply repressed distaste, which had been crystalizing over the years, because his father's peculiar career, as the boy knew only too well, was an object of widespread scorn—and the odium fell upon the son as well.

Trzyniecki's reply to his teenage son was this: "Stefan, you can't ask things like that. Look, if you ask a dying man whether he wants to start life all over again, you can be sure he'll say yes. And he won't ask for reasons to live. It's the same with my work."

This solemn and exhausting work earned no money, so the household was supported by Stefan's mother, or more accurately, by her father. When Stefan learned that Trzyniecki was kept by his wife, he was so outraged that for some time he held his father in contempt. His father's brothers had similar, though less adamant, feelings. But in time the contempt subsided. Anything that lasts too long becomes a matter of indifference. Mrs. Trzyniecki loved her husband, but sadly, everything he did was beyond her understanding. They skirmished, not really knowing why, across the border of two conflicting spheres, workshop and household. Not that his father deliberately turned more and more rooms into workshops. It just happened. Towers of wires and machinery spread over tables, wardrobes, and desks; Stefan's mother trembled for her tablecloths, lace napkins, rhododendrons and cacti; his father did not like plants, secretly tore out their roots, and took a furtive joy when they withered. When cleaning house his mother might throw out a priceless wire or irreplaceable screw. Trzyniecki was off on a distant journey when he worked, and he really returned only during his frequent illnesses. And though Mrs. Trzyniecki felt his sufferings keenly, the fact was that she was most at peace when her husband lay moaning and helpless in bed, enveloped in hot water bottles. At least then she understood what he was talking about and what he was doing.

As Stefan lay there listening to the tolling clock in the darkness above him, his thoughts returned to the day just past. Considered rationally, family ties—those interwoven interests and feelings, that community of births and deaths—seemed somehow sterile and tiresome. He felt a burning impulse to denounce it all, a delirious urge to shout the brutal truth in the faces of his family, to sweep away all the humdrum bustling. But when he searched for the words to address to the living, he remembered Uncle Leszek and froze, as if in terror. Stefan let his thoughts roam independently, as if he were a mere observer. A pleasant weariness came over him, a feeling that sleep was near, and just then he remembered the collective grave in the village cemetery. The vanquished fatherland had perished—a figure of speech. But that soldiers' grave was no figure of speech, and what could he do but stand there in silence, a painful, bittersweet feeling of community greater than individual life and death beating in his heart? And Uncle Leszek nearby. Stefan saw his bare grave, uncovered with snow, as distinctly as if he were already dreaming. But he was not asleep. In his mind the fatherland merged with the family and, though they had been condemned by pure reason, both lived on in him, or perhaps he lived on in them. Well, he didn't know anymore, and as he drifted off to sleep he pressed his hand to his heart, feeling that to free himself from them would be to die.

Staszek

When Stefan opened his eyes, still bleary with sleep, he expected to see the oval mirror on gilt plaster lion's paws that stood by his bed, the bay-front chest of drawers, and the green haze of asparagus out the window. He was surprised to find himself in a large, strange room filled with a clock's sonorous chiming. He was lying very low, just above the floor, and dawn shined through a window frosted over with translucent ice. He could not understand why the old walls of the house next door seemed to be missing.

Only when he sat up and stretched did he recall the previous day's events. He got up quickly, shivering, slipped into the vestibule, and found his coat on the rack. He put it on over his shirt and headed for the bathroom. Candlelight, orange in contrast to the violet light of dawn filtering into the vestibule through the glass of the veranda, shined from behind the unlocked door. Someone was in the bathroom. Stefan recognized Uncle Ksawery's voice and immediately felt an urge to eavesdrop. He justified his curiosity on psychological grounds: he believed that there was a single, ultimate truth about people that could be discovered by watching them when they were alone.

He walked quietly to the bathroom and, without touching the door, peered inside through a crack as wide as his hand.

Two candles burned on the glass shelf. Clouds of steam, yellow in the light, rose from the tub against the wall and enveloped the ghostly figure of his uncle who, dressed in homespun pants and a Ukrainian-style shirt, was shaving, making strange grimaces into the dripping mirror, and declaiming emphatically, but with a caution demanded by the razor, an obscene limerick.

Stefan, somewhat disenchanted, stood there wondering what to do when his uncle, as if he had felt his gaze (or perhaps he simply spotted him in the mirror), said in a totally different voice, without turning, "How are you, Stefan? It's you, isn't it? Come on in, you can wash. There's enough hot water."

Stefan said good morning to his uncle and obediently entered the bathroom. He washed hurriedly, somewhat inhibited by the presence of Ksawery, who went on shaving, not paying any attention to him. There was silence for a moment, until his uncle said, "Stefan."

"Yes, Uncle?"

"Do you know how it happened?"

Stefan understood from his tone what Ksawery meant, but, reluctant to admit it, he asked, "With Uncle Leszek, you mean?"

Ksawery, shaving his upper lip, did not answer. After a long silence, he spoke abruptly: "He came here on the second of August. He was going fishing for trout there below the mill. You know the place. Naturally he didn't say a word. I knew him so well. We had duck for dinner, just like yesterday. But with apples, which I don't have anymore. The soldiers took them all in September. And he didn't want any duck. He always liked duck. That made me wonder. And he had that face. Except it's hardest to notice in someone close to you. A man won't admit to himself that . . ."

"An aversion to meat, cachexia?" Stefan asked, realizing that he sounded ridiculous. His own knowledge somehow shamed him, even as it gave him a certain satisfaction. He stood up and dried himself quickly, not quite thoroughly, because he could sense what his uncle was going to say and he didn't want to have to hear it naked. Because it made him feel defenseless? He didn't try to decide. Ksawery was still looking in the mirror, his back to Stefan, and he went on without answering the question.

"He didn't want to be examined. And I was terrible. I made jokes, said I was studying ticklishness, that I wanted to see if his belly was bigger than mine, stuff like that. It was a tumor the size of a fist, so hard you couldn't even move it, metastasized and everything, hell . . ."

"Carcinoma scirrhosum," Stefan said quietly, though he had no idea why. The Latin term for cancer was like an exorcism, a scientific spell that removed the uncertainty, the dread, the trembling, giving it the precision and tranquility of the inevitable.

"A textbook case," Uncle Ksawery mumbled as he shaved the same spot on his cheek over and over. Stefan stood motionless at the door, wrapped in the short bathrobe, his trousers in his hand. What else could he do? He listened.

"Did you know he almost became a doctor? You didn't? Well, he quit after the fourth year of medical school. He'd been an intern for a couple of years. We even started medical school at the same time, because I frittered away a couple of years after high school graduation. All because of a . . . well, never mind. Anyway, when he watched me examine him, he knew what it was. And I knew it was too late to operate, but when you're a doctor the only other place you can send somebody is the undertaker's. It's never too late for that. What the hell, I thought, God knows what kind of pain he's got. He agreed right off. I went to Hrubiński. A son of a bitch, but hands of gold. He agreed to operate but for dollars, because things were so uncertain and the złoty might go to hell. When he looked at the X rays he refused point-blank, but I begged him."

Ksawery turned to Stefan, looked at him as if he were holding back a laugh, and asked, "Have you ever got down on your knees to anybody, Stefan?" He quickly added, "I don't mean in church."

"No."

"Well, that's what I did. Got down on my knees. You don't believe it? Well I did, I'm telling you. Hrubiński operated on September twelfth. The German tanks were already in Topolów. The oats in the field were burning. The nurses had fled, so I was his assistant. The first time in years. He opened him up, sewed him up, and left. He was furious. I wasn't surprised. But he cursed me. Everything was absurd that whole September, everywhere, and Poland, well . . ."

Ksawery began sharpening his straight-razor on a belt, deliberately, slower and slower, and without stopping he said, "Right before the operation, after the scopolamine, Leszek said, 'This is the end, isn't it?' So naturally I started talking the way you talk to a patient. But he meant Poland, he wasn't talking about himself. I should go to his grave and tell him that Poland will rise again. A dreamer he was. But who knows how to die anyway? When he woke up after the operation, I was with him and he asked what time it was. Like an idiot I told him the truth. I should have set the clock ahead, because with his medical training he knew that a radical operation has to last an hour at the very least, and this was all over in fifteen minutes. So he knew . . ."

27

"What happened then?" Stefan asked, not really wanting to know, just to fill a menacing silence.

"Afterward I took him to Anzelm's, that's where he wanted to go. I didn't see him for three months, not until December. But that's something I never understood." Uncle Ksawery, moving slowly, blindly, put the razor down and, standing next to Stefan, stared as if seeing something unusual at his feet. "He was in bed, he looked like a skeleton. He could barely swallow milk, his voice was frail, a blind man could see the state he was in, but he . . . how can I put it? He was completely confident. He explained away everything, and I mean everything. He rationalized. The operation had been a success, he was getting stronger every day, he was getting better, soon he would be up and around again. He had his hands and legs massaged. Every morning he told Aniela how he felt, and she wrote it down for the doctor so he could treat him properly. Meanwhile, the tumor was the size of a loaf of bread. But he told them to keep his belly bandaged so he couldn't touch it, as if to protect the scar. The illness he didn't talk about, except to say that it had been just a minor thing, or even that there was nothing wrong with him anymore."

"Do you think he was . . . abnormal?" Stefan asked in a whisper.

"Normal! Abnormal! What does that have to do with it? He was a normal dying man! He couldn't tear the cancer out of his body, so he tore it out of his memory. Maybe he was lying, maybe he really believed it, maybe he just wanted others to believe. How should I know which? He said that he was feeling better and better, and cried more and more often."

"He cried?" Stefan asked with childlike fear, remembering how strong Uncle Leszek looked on horseback, holding a double-barreled shotgun pointed at the ground.

"Yes. And do you know why? They prescribed morphine

suppositories for the pain, and he was putting them in himself. But when the nurse had to, he broke down. 'I can't do anything myself,' he said, 'except put that suppository in, and now they take that away.' He couldn't get up, but he said he didn't want to. When they gave him milk, he'd say it wasn't worth waking up for, that it would be different if it was broth, but when they gave him broth, he didn't want that either. God, being with him then, talking to him! He'd hold his hands up, they looked like twigs, and he'd say, 'Look, I'm putting on weight.' He got incredibly suspicious. 'What are you whispering about?' 'What did the doctor really say?' Finally, Aunt Skoczyńska got the priest. He showed up with the oil for extreme unction and I thought, oh no, what now, but Leszek took it in perfect calm. Except that later the same night he started whispering. I thought he was talking in his sleep, so I didn't answer. But he whispered louder: 'Ksaw, do something.' I went closer, and again: 'Ksaw, do something.' You're a doctor, Stefan, aren't you? So you know I had the morphine all ready, just in case he wanted . . . I had the right dose with me, you know, carried it in my shirt pocket all the time. That night, I thought he wanted me to . . . you understand. But when I looked into his eyes, I realized that he wanted to live. So I didn't do anything, and he said it again: 'Ksaw, do something.' The same thing over and over, until dawn. He didn't say anything else, and then I had to leave. Well, yesterday Aniela told me that on the last night she went to take a nap and when she came back to see him, he was dead. But he was lying the wrong way."

"What do you mean, the wrong way?" Stefan whispered in uncomprehending dread.

"The wrong way. With his feet at the head. Why? I have no idea. I guess he wanted to do something, something to stay alive."

Standing there in his wrinkled pants, his shirt open at the chest and traces of soap on his face, Uncle Ksawery slowly lowered his head. Then he looked at Stefan. His quick black eyes were sharp and hot.

"I'm telling you this because you're a doctor. It's something you should know! I don't know why, but I almost prayed. Unbelievable what a man can be driven to!"

Water dripped off the mirror and onto the floor. They both jerked when the drawing-room clock struck, loud, majestic, and deliberate.

Uncle Ksawery turned back to the basin and began splashing water on his face and neck, spitting loudly, snorting water out his nostrils. Stefan dressed hurriedly and somehow furtively, then slipped out of the bathroom without a word.

In the dining room the table was already set. Blue icicles outside the window absorbed the day's brightness and sent golden flashes through the panes and onto the glass of the grandfather clock, breaking into rainbows on the cut-glass carafe on the table. Uncle Anzelm, Trzyniecki from Kielce with his daughter, Great-aunt Skoczyńska, and Aunt Aniela came in one by one.

There was a big pot of coffee on the table, a loaf of bread, pats of butter, honey. They ate in near-silence, everyone somehow subdued, looking at the sunny window and exchanging monosyllables. Stefan was careful to avoid getting the skin of the milk in his coffee. He hated that. Uncle Anzelm was thoughtful and gruff. Nothing really happened, but it took an effort to sit at the table. Stefan glanced once or twice at Uncle Ksawery, the last to appear, with no tie, his black jacket unbuttoned. Stefan felt that a secret covenant had been concluded between them, but his uncle ignored his meaningful glances, rolled pieces of bread into little balls and dropped them on the table. Then one of the village women who was helping out came in and announced loudly to the entire room, "A gentleman is here to see the younger Mr. Trzyniecki."

That formal "younger Mr. Trzyniecki" reflected the efforts of Uncle Leszek, who had always drilled the help when he stayed at Ksawery's. Stefan, taken by surprise, bolted from the table, mumbled an excuse, and ran for the hallway. It was bright there, and with the light streaming through the glass of the veranda he could not make out the newcomer's face, just his silhouette against the glare. The stranger was wearing an overcoat, holding his cap, and it took Stefan a moment to recognize him.

"Staszek! What are you doing here—I wasn't expecting you."

He led the guest into the drawing room and almost violently pulled the fur-collared coat off him. He took it to the vestibule, came back, sat his guest in an armchair, and pulled up a chair for himself. "So, how are you? What's new? Where've you been staying?"

Stanisław Krzeczotek, a classmate of Stefan's at the university, smiled with a mixture of confusion and satisfaction. He was a little taken aback by Stefan's animation. "Well, nothing much. I'm working not far from here, in Bierzyniec. Yesterday I happened to hear about the funeral, I mean, that your uncle . . ." He paused for a second, avoiding Stefan's gaze, then went on. "So I thought I might find you here. It's been a long time, hasn't it?"

"Yes, a long time," Stefan said. "You're working in Bierzyniec? No kidding! What are you, a district doctor? But Uncle Ksawery . . ."

"No, I'm working in the asylum. With Pajączkowski. Come on, you know the place."

"Oh, the asylum. You mean you're a psychiatrist? That's a surprise."

31

"For me, too, but there was a vacancy, and an advertisement by the Medical Association . . . before September, you know."

Krzeczotek began explaining how he came to be in Bierzyniec. He told the story in his usual way: slowly, with innumerable unimportant details. As always, Stefan got impatient and urged him along with questions that ran ahead of the narrative. And all the while he looked at his friend with unconcealed delight. They had met in the first year of medical school, brought together by their mutual lack of enthusiasm for working with cadavers. Staszek lived near Stefan and suggested that they study together, since textbooks cost so much and it was not easy to study alone for long periods. Stefan had noticed Staszek, but had not approached him, sensing a touch of the star pupil in him, something he couldn't stand. It wasn't until they had been to some dances and parties together that he started to trust him. Staszek was always the life of the party. Once he got to know him better, though, Stefan realized that the boisterousness and cheer were only on the surface. Staszek was so full of anxieties, he could never make up his mind about anything. Examinations, classmates, cadavers, professors, women—he was afraid of everything. With great skill he had devised himself a mask of merriment, which he discarded with relief whenever he could. Stefan was especially fascinated to discover that although girls liked Staszek and laughed at his jokes, he could charm them only in a group. Even with just two girls he did well enough, bouncing back and forth between them with clever flirtation, but with only one girl he was hopeless. There comes a time when you have to forget the jokes and become serious, but Staszek just couldn't do it. Everyone realized that dancing, flirting, and light banter were a sort of preparatory action, like a peacock reading its tail for the peahen. But that was as far as Staszek's social talents went.

Stefan discovered this by tracing his friend's amazing transformations: leaving a gathering where he had sparkled, he turned silent and morose. This was followed by long talks between the two of them, autumn walks in the park, evenings spent wrestling with philosophical conundrums: heated arguments, efforts to find "the ultimate truth" or "the meaning of life" and similar ontological deliberations. Neither of them was capable of such incisive reasoning on his own. They catalyzed, complemented each other. But not in personal matters. Staszek propounded a theory to explain his erotic defeats: he did not believe in love. He liked to read about love, but did not believe in its existence. "Look," he said, "just read Abderhalden! If you inject a female monkey with prolactin and stick a puppy in the cage with her, she immediately starts caressing it and taking care of it. But two or three days later she'll eat the beloved doggie. That's mother love for you, the most sublime of all feelings—a few chemicals in the blood!"

Secretly Stefan felt superior to his classmate. Staszek had a round, plump moon-face, though his body was thin. He had a good-humored potato nose, the tip constantly plagued by a big pimple. He froze in winter because he considered going without long underwear a sign of manhood. And he spent three-quarters of every year hopelessly, obviously, and comically in love. They spoke a great deal about life in general, but very little about their own lives. Yet now, sitting on the damask seat-covers in Uncle Ksawery's shadowy drawing room, it was hard to plunge straight into the refuge of philosophizing. When Staszek finished his story, there was an uncomfortable silence. In an effort to break it, he asked Stefan about his professional life.

"Me? Well, for the moment I'm not doing anything. Not working anywhere. And with the Germans now, the Occupation, I don't know. I'm looking. I'll have to find some position somewhere, but I haven't really thought about it too specifically yet," Stefan said, speaking more and more slowly as he went on. They both fell silent again. Stefan was disappointed at how little they had to say to each other, and desperately sought a subject. More to keep the conversation going than out of any real curiosity, he asked, "So how is it in the asylum? Do you like it there?"

"Ah, the asylum."

Staszek perked up and seemed about to say something, when suddenly he stopped, his eyes wide, and his face lit up. "Stefan, listen! I just thought of it right now, but so what? Archimedes also, you know! Listen, why don't you come to work at the asylum? Why not? It's a good place, you'd get some specialization, you know the area here, it would be quiet, interesting work, and you'd have plenty of time to do research—I remember you always wanted to do research."

"Me? The asylum?" Stefan asked in amazement. "Just like that? I only came here for the funeral, you know. But it really doesn't matter to me . . ." He stopped, not sure whether the last words sounded wrong, but Staszek hadn't noticed anything. They spent the next fifteen minutes going over the subject, discussing what it would be like if Stefan took the position, because there was indeed an opening for a doctor at the asylum. Staszek answered Stefan's doubts one after the other: "So what if you didn't specialize in psychiatry? Nobody's born a specialist. Your colleagues would be first class, believe me! Well actually I guess doctors are like everybody else—some better, some worse. But they're all interesting. And it's such an easy place! It's like being outside the Occupation, in fact it's even like being outside the world!" Staszek got so excited that he turned the asylum into a kind of extraterrestrial observatory, a delicious solitude in which a man naturally endowed with a fine intellect could develop in peace. They talked and talked, Stefan totally unconvinced that anything would come of it but nonetheless encouraging his friend for fear of the vacuum that beckoned beyond the borders of this last topic.

There was a knock at the door. Uncle Anzelm and the aunts were leaving for the station. By rights, Stefan should have gone with them, but he managed to get out with a frantic kissing of hands and a barrage of bows. Aunt Aniela seemed to be in a good mood, which under different circumstances would have upset Stefan—he remembered what Ksawery had told him—but he was in too much of a hurry to get back to Staszek to be indignant. This renewed, albeit final contact with the family—Anzelm's arrogance as he put his arms around Stefan for a kiss but only brushed his face with a stubbly cheek, the idiotic injunctions and advice of Aunt Melania— made Staszek's proposition seem much more attractive. But when he returned to find his friend gazing at the old engravings on the drawing-room wall with affected nonchalance, he felt uncertain again. In the end, after carefully considering the pros and cons, he announced that he would go home to settle certain things (this was a fiction, there was nothing to settle, but it sounded plausible). Then—after a certain length of time (he emphasized this, so as not to look too much like a swine afterward)—he would come back to Bierzyniec.

At noon Stefan bid his uncle a polite but reserved farewell and left for the station. Staszek went with him; he could take the same train as far as Bierzyniec.

It was a warm spring-like day. The melting snow made gurgling streams that turned the road into a quagmire. Stefan and Staszek said little as they slogged along, partly because negotiating the puddles demanded attention, but also because there was nothing to say. They killed time at the station, smoking cigarettes the way they used to between lectures, the lighted ends cupped in their hands, until the train came. As

35

the train pulled in, Staszek looked at it aghast and decided to go on foot. The cars were bursting with people. They were pressed against the windows, sitting on the roofs, hanging on to every rail, handle, and step. When the train stopped and was invaded by the mob of peasants and shoppers waiting to get on, it was an outright battle. Stefan vented an aggression he would not have expected of himself, pushing and shoving among the sheepskins as if his life depended on it. The train was already moving when he obtained a toehold on the edge of a wooden step. With both hands he grabbed the overcoats and furs of the people hanging from the door above him. But when he realized that he would not last more than a few minutes in that position, he jumped. The train was moving so fast that he nearly fell, but somehow he escaped with no more than a good spray of dirty snow and slush. When he turned from the tracks, flushed with effort and anger, he saw Staszek's indulgent, amiable smile. This only fanned his anger, but his friend called from a distance, "Take it easy, Stefan. It's fate, not me. Come on, we'll walk to Bierzyniec together."

Stefan stood there indecisive for a moment and was about to say something—not about the vague things he had to "settle," but about clean clothes and soap. With an energy unusual for him, Staszek took him by the arm and told him that at the asylum he would find whatever he needed, and he did it so warmly that Stefan smiled, waved away his reservations, and slopped through the mud with his friend toward the three humps of the Bierzyniec Hills that loomed brightly on the horizon.

The Genius

From Nieczawy to Bierzyniec it was twelve kilometers of winding, sodden clay road. When they reached the top of the highest
hill, the road dropped into a deep channel that led through a
narrower but equally marshy passage until a gentle rise with
young forest on the southern slope suddenly appeared from
behind a clump of trees. Massive buildings ringed by a brick
wall loomed on the ridge. An asphalt road led up to the main
gate. Out of breath after their brisk hike, they stopped a few
hundred meters short of their goal. From this height Stefan
had a view of a wide, gently rolling space with fog creeping
in here and there in the setting sun. The melting snow reflected
strange colors. A notched stone arch with an indistinct inscription, both its ends hidden in bushes, rose in front of the
black gate. When they got closer, Stefan made out the words
CHRISTO TRANSFIGURATO.

Hastily crunching through puddles still frozen in shady
spots, they reached the gate. A fat, bearded porter let them
in. Staszek went into feverish but subdued action. He ordered
Stefan to wait in an empty room on the ground floor while he
looked for the head doctor. Stefan paced the flagstone floor

staring vacantly at the patterns of a fresco partly covered by plaster; there was a sort of pale gold halo and, just where the blue plaster began, a mouth opened as if to scream or sing. He turned around when he heard steps. Staszek, already wearing a long white smock with cuffs beginning to fray from too much laundering, had returned sooner than he expected. He looked taller and thinner in the smock, and his round face beamed with satisfaction.

"Perfect," he said, taking Stefan by the arm. "I've already talked everything over with Pajpak. He's our boss. His name is Pajączkowski, but he stutters, so . . . but you must be hungry, admit it! Don't worry, we'll take care of everything right away."

The doctors roomed in a separate building, attractive, cozy and bright. Comfort of a high order was the rule. In the room Staszek brought him to, Stefan found hot running water and a sink, a bed with something clinical about it, light, somewhat austere furniture, and even three snowdrops in a glass on the table. But the most important thing was the absence of the smell of iodine or any other hospital odors. As Staszek chattered on without stopping to take a breath, Stefan tried the spigots, inspected the bathroom, tested the delightfully roaring shower, came back into the room, drank coffee with milk, smeared something yellow and salty on a roll and ate it—all out of friendship, so that Staszek could savor the fruits of his provident care.

"Well? What do you think?" Staszek asked when Stefan had finally examined everything and finished eating.

"Of what?"

"Of everything. The world."

"Is that an invitation to philosophize?" Stefan said, unable to hold back his laughter.

"What do you mean, philosophize? The world—these days,

that means the Germans. Everybody says they'll get it in the end, but I'm not so sure, I'm sorry to say. They're already talking about management changes—apparently a Pole can't be director. But nothing's settled yet. Anyway, first of all you have to get to know the place. Then you can choose a department. There's no hurry. Take a good look first."

It occurred to Stefan that Staszek sounded just like Aunt Skoczyńska, but he only asked, "Where are . . . they?"

Through the window he could see misty flower beds, indistinct pavilions, and a tower in the distance, Turkish or Moorish, he wasn't sure which.

"You'll see them, don't worry. They're all over. But relax. You won't be going on the wards today. I'll explain it all to you, so you won't get lost. This, my friend, is a madhouse."

"I know."

"I don't think you do. You took a psychiatry course and observed one patient, a neurological case, true?"

"Yes."

"So you see. Therapy? Nothing to it. Under the age of forty, a lunatic has dementia praecox. Cold baths, bromine, and scopolamine. Over forty, dementia senilis. Scopolamine, bromine, and cold showers. And electroshock. That's all there is to psychiatry. But here we are just a tiny island in a really weird sea. I'm telling you, if it wasn't for the personnel . . . Anyway, you'll pick it up soon enough. It would be worth it to spend your life here. And not necessarily as a doctor."

"As a patient, you mean?"

"As a guest. We have guests too. You can meet some eminent people here. Don't laugh, I'm serious."

"Such as?"

"Sekułowski."

"The poet? The one who . . . ."

"Yes, he's here with us, more or less. That is, how should

39

I put it? A drug addict. Morphine, cocaine, peyote even, but he's off that now. He's staying here, as if he was on vacation. Hiding from the Germans, in other words. He writes all day, and not poems either. Philosophical thunderbolts. You'll see! Look, I have evening rounds now. I'll see you in half an hour."

Staszek left. Stefan stood at the window for a while, then walked around his new quarters again. He was somehow taking everything in, not by consciously focusing on objects, but just by standing there, passive. He felt a new layer of sensations settling over the experiences of the past few days, a geology of memory taking shape, a sunken lower stratum made of dreams, and an upper stratum, more fluid, susceptible to the influences of the outside world.

He stood in front of the mirror, looking intently at his own face. His forehead could have been higher, he thought, and his hair more definite, either completely blond or brown. Only his beard was really dark, making him look as though he always needed a shave. Then there were his eyes—some people called them chestnut, others brown. He was indeterminate. Except for the nose he had inherited from his father: sharp and hooked, "a greedy nose," his mother called it. He relaxed and then tensed his face so that his features looked more noble. One grimace led to another, and he made face after face until finally he spun away and walked to the window.

"If I could just stop aping myself!" he thought angrily. "I should become a pragmatist. Action, action, action." He remembered something his father used to say: "A man who has no goal in life must create one for himself." It was better to have a whole set of goals, short- and long-term. Not vague ones like "be brave" or "be good," but things like "fix the toilet." He longed intensely for the lot of a simple person.

"God! If only I could plow, sow, reap, and plow again. Or hammer stools together or weave baskets and carry them to

40

market." The career of a village sculptor whittling saints or of a potter baking a red-glazed rooster struck him as the pinnacle of happiness. Peace. Simplicity. A tree would be a tree, period. None of that idiotic, pointless, exhausting thinking: Why the hell does it grow, what does it mean that it's alive, why are there plants, why is it what it is and not something else, is the soul made of atoms? Just to be able to stop for once! He started pacing, getting more and more annoyed. Luckily, Staszek came back from his rounds. Stefan suspected that Staszek felt confident in this hospital, like a one-eyed man among the blind. He was a gentle lunatic, a lunatic on a small scale, and so must seem uncommonly well-adjusted in this background of raving madness.

The doctors' dining room was on the top floor next to a large billiards room and a smaller room with what looked like card tables.

The food wasn't bad: ground meat and grits with bean salad, followed by crisp bliny. Jugs of coffee at the end.

"War, my friend, *à la guerre comme à la guerre*," said Stefan's neighbor to his left. Stefan observed the company. As usual when he saw new faces, they seemed undifferentiated, interchangeable, devoid of character.

The man who had made the crack about war—Doctor Dygier or Rygier, he had introduced himself unclearly—was short, with a big nose, dark face, and a deep scar in his forehead. He wore a small pince-nez with a golden frame, which kept slipping. He adjusted it with an automatic gesture that began to get on Stefan's nerves. They spoke in low murmurs about indifferent subjects: whether winter had ended, whether they would run out of coal, whether there would be a lot of work, how much they were being paid. Doctor Rygier (not Dygier) took tiny sips of coffee, chose the most well-done bliny, and spoke through his nose, saying little of interest. As they spoke, they both watched Professor Pajączkowski. The old man, who looked like a dove chick with his sparse, feathery beard through which the pink skin underneath was visible, was tiny, had wrinkled hands with a slight tremor, stuttered occasionally, slurped his coffee, and shook his head when he began to speak.

"So, you would like to work with us?" he asked Stefan, shaking his head.

"Yes, I would."

"Well certainly, certainly."

"Because the practice . . . it would be most useful," Stefan murmured. He felt a strong aversion to old men, official meetings, and boring conversation, and here he had all three at once.

"Well, we will . . . yes . . . exactly . . ." Pajpak went on, shaking his head again.

Beside him sat a tall, thin doctor wearing a dustcoat stained with silver nitrate. Strikingly but not unpleasantly ugly, he had a harelip scar, a flat nose, wide lips, and a yellow smile. When he put his hands on the table, Stefan was amazed by their size and handsome shape. He considered two things important, the shape of the fingernails and the proportions of the hand's width and length, and on both counts Doctor Marglewski revealed a good pedigree.

There was one woman at the table. Stefan had noticed her when he came in. When they shook hands, her hand was surprisingly cold, narrow, and muscular. The thought of being caressed by that hand was unpleasant and exciting at the same time.

Doctor Nosilewska (Miss? Mrs.?) had a pale face enveloped in a storm of chestnut hair that burned with gold and honey highlights. Below her lucid arched forehead her eyebrows tilted toward her temples like wings above sharp blue eyes that seemed almost electric. She was a perfect beauty, which meant that she was almost invisible—there was no birthmark or mole to capture the eye. Her tranquility was tinged with the maternal touch that marked Aphrodite's features, but her smile was enlivened by the glints in her hair, her eyes, and a small depression in her left cheek—not a dimple, but a playful hint of one.

There was also a younger doctor with a pimply face, dark hair, and a hooked nose. Nobody spoke to him. His name was Kuśniewicz.

Stefan gathered from the conversation that the work was demanding but interesting, that psychiatry, however tedious, was the finest of callings, although given the choice, most of those present would have changed specialties. The patients were awful even when peaceful and quiet, and should all be given shock therapy whether they needed it or not. No one said anything about politics. It was like being on the ocean floor: all motion was indolent and subdued, and the most powerful of storms on the surface would be felt here only as a ripple, cause for a professional diagnosis.

The next day Stefan found out that he had not met all the doctors. He was accompanying Doctor Nosilewska on morning rounds (he had been assigned to the women's ward), and as they walked along a gravel path spotted with water from the dripping trees, they met a tall man in a white coat. The encounter was brief enough, but it engraved the man in Stefan's memory. He had ugly yellow features that seemed chiseled in ivory, eyes screened by dark glasses, a large pointed nose, and thin lips that were stretched across his teeth. He reminded Stefan of a reproduction he had once seen of the mummy of Ramses II: an asceticism independent of age, features somehow timeless. His wrinkles did not indicate the years he had lived, but seemed to belong to the sculpture of his face. The doctor,

43

who was the best surgeon in the asylum, was rail-thin and flat-footed. His feet were wide apart as he slopped through the mud, and after a perfunctory bow to Nosilewska, he trotted up the outside spiral staircase of the red pavilion.

Nosilewska held in her white hand the key that opened the doors between wards. Almost all the buildings were connected by long glass-topped galleries so that doctors on their rounds would not be exposed to frost and rain. These galleries were reminiscent of greenhouse antechambers. But that impression vanished inside the wards. All the walls were pale blue. There were no spigots, drains, plugs, or door handles—just smooth walls to the ceiling. Patients in cherry robes and clacking clogs strolled up and down the cold, bright rooms between rows of neat beds made up in what seemed a military style. The windows were discreetly barred or covered with screens behind wide flower boxes.

Nosilewska walked through the wards locking doors behind her and opening new ones with fluid, automatic, almost somnolent movements. Stefan had a key too, now, but could not handle it so deftly.

Faces loomed around him: some pale and drawn, as if shrunken down to the skull, others puffy, swollen, unhealthily flushed. The men's individuality was erased by their shaved heads. The bumps and oddities of their denuded skulls were so ugly that they overwhelmed the expressions on their faces. Protruding ears, extreme myopia, or a gaze fixed on a random object—these were the patients' most obvious features, at least at first glance. A male nurse was pushing a patient along in the corridor, his movements not brutal so much as inappropriate for dealing with a human being. They softened for a moment as Stefan and Nosilewska passed. There was a gentle cry somewhere in the distance, as if someone was shouting out of conviction, rather than compulsion or illness, as if practicing.

44

Nosilewska herself seemed strange. Stefan had noticed it earlier that morning. At breakfast, he had tried to memorize her features out of aesthetic interest, so that he could summon them up later. He noticed then that her eyes seemed vacant, staring at nothing, as she bent her head like a swan's over the rim of a steaming mug. He watched all her other unconscious signs of life: the delicate pulse at the base of her neck, the peaceful clouding of her eyes, the trembling of her lashes. When she slowly turned her blue, piercing gaze on him, he was almost frightened, and a moment later he quickly drew his leg back when their knees touched—the contact struck him as dangerous.

Nosilewska had a neat office in the women's ward. Though it contained no personal objects, a femininity more subtle than any perfume hung in the air. They sat at a white metal desk and Nosilewska took a card index from a drawer. Like all female doctors, she could not use nail polish, but the short, round ornamental shaping of her fingertips was boyishly beautiful. High on the wall hung a small black Christ, suspended from two disproportionately massive hooks. That fascinated Stefan, but he had to pay attention: she was giving him a rundown of his duties. Her voice seemed close to breaking, as if she were about to speak in a high-pitched trill. Stefan had never written a case history of a psychiatric examination; in medical school he had copied, of course. When he found that he would not have to start one from scratch but would be adding to old notes, he appreciated Nosilewska's helpful suggestions. She understood, as he did, that all the writing was infernally boring and futile, but that it had to be done out of respect for tradition.

"So that's it."

He thanked her and got ready to try it himself. Later he wondered whether that elegant woman in sheer white stockings and the tailored white coat with gray mother-of-pearl buttons realized what a set piece they were playing out. She rang for the nurse, a stocky, towheaded girl.

"Usually you walk around and ask the patients how they are, and what they think about their—well, symptoms, you know what I mean? But right now I'd like to give you a tour of part of my kingdom."

It was indeed her kingdom. Though he was not claustrophobic, he was keenly and unpleasantly aware of all the doors that had been locked behind him with the magic key. Bars darkened the window even here in the office, and behind the medicine locker, in the corner, lay a wrinkled fabric: a straitjacket. The patient who was brought in was grotesquely deformed by pajama bottoms too long and tight. She wore black slippers. Her face was expressionless, but seemed to conceal some surprise. With makeup, she might have passed for attractive. Her eyebrows had been artificially blackened, apparently with coal. They extended all the way to her temples. This might have accounted for the sense of strangeness, but Stefan was so surprised by what she said, he had difficulty looking at her. She was asked in a subdued, uninterested way whether there was anything new. She smiled promisingly and replied in a reedy, melodic voice, "I had a visitor."

"Who was it, Suzanna?"

"The Lord Jesus. He came at night."

"Really?"

"Yes. He crawled into my bed and . . ." And she described sexual intercourse in the most vulgar terms, looking curiously at Stefan, as if to say, "And what do you think of that?"

Stefan froze and was so embarrassed that he didn't know where to look. Nosilewska took out a small cigarette case, offered him one, took one for herself, and began asking the patient for details. Stefan's hands shook so much as he tried to light her cigarette that he broke three matches. When No-

46

silewska asked him to check the patient's reflexes, he did it awkwardly. Then the nurse, who had been standing by impassively, took the patient by the arm, lifted her out of her chair like a sack of laundry, and led her out.

"Paranoia," said Nosilewska. "She has frequent hallucinations. You don't have to write it all down, of course, but a few words would be in order."

The next patient, a fat woman with reddish-gray hair, made countless fidgety gestures, as if trying to break free of the girl who held her from behind by the folds of her robe. She talked nonstop, a stream of nonsensically strung-together words that flowed on even when the doctor was asking her a question. Suddenly she jerked more violently, and despite himself Stefan flinched. Nosilewska ordered her taken away.

The third patient was barely human. A thick, cloying stench preceded her. It would not have been easy to guess the sex of the tall, wretched creature. Bluish skin on a shriveled frame showed through the holes in her robe. Her face was large, bony, and blunt as a scarecrow's. Nosilewska said something Stefan couldn't catch, and the patient, who had been standing stiffly with her arms at her sides, began to speak.

"Menin aeide thea . . ." She was reciting the *Iliad*, accenting the hexameters properly.

After the nurse took the patient away, Nosilewska told Stefan, "She has a Ph.D. For a while she was catatonic. I wanted you to see her, because she's pretty much a textbook case: perfectly preserved memory."

Stefan couldn't help saying, "But the way she looked . . ."

"It's not our fault. I used to give her clean clothes, but a few hours later she'd look exactly the same. You can't have a nurse standing over every coprophagic, especially these days. I'm going over to the pharmacy now, but you write out the case histories. Enter the dates and numbers in the book.

Unfortunately, we have to take care of that administrative formality ourselves."

Stefan yearned to ask whether the sort of obscenity the first patient had used was common, but the question would have revealed his inexperience, so he held his tongue. Nosilewska left. He riffled through the papers. When he was finished, he had to force himself to get up and leave. Women were walking around. Some were giggling as they dressed up with scraps of paper, strips of rag, and string. In the corner was a bed with screens at the side and cords across the top. It was empty. As Stefan walked along the wall, instinctively trying to keep his back to the patients, he heard a scream of despair. He looked through a thick portal set into a small door. It was an isolation cell. The naked woman inside was throwing her body against the padded walls as if it were a sack. Her eyes met Stefan's and she froze. For an instant she was a normal human being, ashamed of her terrible situation and her nakedness. Then she seemed to murmur something and came closer. When her face was up against the glass, her long gray hair falling across it, she opened her bruised lips and licked the pane with her lacerated tongue, leaving streaks of pink-tinged saliva.

Stefan fled, unable to control himself. He heard a scream. In a bathroom, a nurse was trying to force a howling and fiercely struggling patient into a tub. Her legs glowed bright red: the water was too hot. Stefan told the nurse to make it cooler. He knew he had been too polite, but he felt he could not reprimand her. It was too soon for that, he thought.

A third room was filled with snoring, rattling, and wheezing. Women suffering from insulin shock lay in bed, covered with dark blankets. Here and there a pale blue eye followed Stefan with an insect's vacant gaze. Someone's fingers clutched his smock. Back in the corridor, he ran into Staszek.

Stefan's face must have looked different, because his friend

48

slapped him on the shoulder and said, "So how was it? For God's sake don't take it all so seriously." He noticed wet stains under Stefan's arms.

With relief Stefan told him about what the first patient said and how the others looked. It had been so horrible.

"Don't be childish," Staszek said. "It's only the symptoms of disease."

"I want to get out of here."

"The women are always worse. I was just talking to Pajpak, because I could see it coming." Stefan noticed with satisfaction that Staszek was using his influence. "But Nosilewska really is all alone here, and she needs help. Stay with her a week to make it look good, and then we'll get you transferred to Rygier. Or maybe—wait a minute, that's an idea. You assisted Włostowski as an anesthesiologist, didn't you?"

In fact, Stefan had been good at anesthesia.

"The thing is, Kauters has been complaining that he doesn't have anybody."

"Who?"

"Doctor Orybald Kauters," Staszek intoned. "Interesting name, isn't it? He looks Egyptian, but supposedly he's descended from the Courlandian nobility. A neurosurgeon. And not bad."

"Yes, that would be better," Stefan said. "At least I'd learn something. Because here . . ." he waved his hand.

"I wanted to warn you earlier, but there was no time. The nurses are completely unqualified, so they are a little callous, a little brutal. In fact, they do some pretty rotten things."

Stefan interrupted to tell him about the nurse who almost scalded a patient.

"Yes, that happens. You have to keep an eye on them, but basically—well, you know how people are. Behind one's choice of a profession, there can be aberrant emotions . . ."

"There's an interesting question," Stefan said. He was look-ing for an excuse not to go back to the ward and wanted to talk. They were standing under a corridor window. "A free choice of professions sounds like a good thing," he said, "but really it's only the law of random distribution in a large pop-ulation that guarantees that all important social positions will be filled. Theoretically, it could happen that no one would want to work in the sewers, for example. Then what? Would they be drafted?"

"It's worked so far. The random distribution hasn't failed. Actually, this is one of Pajpak's favorite themes. I'll have to tell him." Staszek smiled, showing teeth yellowed by nicotine. "He says it's a good thing people are so unintelligent. 'Nothing but university professors—that would be a n-n-nightmare. Who would sweep the streets?' " Staszek intoned, imitating the old man's voice.

But Stefan was getting bored with this too.

"Will you come back to the ward with me? I want to take the case histories up to my room. I guess one should be able to write in the ward, but I can't with that door behind me."

"What door?"

"I keep feeling they're standing behind me, looking through the keyhole."

"Hang a towel over the door," Staszek said so matter-of-factly that Stefan felt reassured: Staszek must have gone through the same thing.

"No, I'd rather do it this way."

They went back to the duty room, and to get there they had to pass through the three women's rooms. A tall blonde with a ruined, terrified face called Stefan aside as if he was a stranger she was asking for help on the street instead of a doctor.

"I see you're new here," she whispered, looking around

50

nervously. "Can I talk to you for five minutes? Even two?" she begged. Stefan looked at Staszek, who stood smiling slightly, playing with a neurological rubber hammer.

"Doctor, I'm completely normal!"

Stefan knew that dissimulation was a classic symptom in some forms of madness, so he thought he knew how to handle her. "We'll talk about it during rounds."

"We will? Really?" She seemed to cheer up. "I can see you understand me, doctor."

Then she leaned close and whispered, "Because there's nothing but lunatics here. *Nothing*," she added with emphasis.

He wondered why she had been so secretive. Who else did she expect to find in an asylum? But as he walked with Staszek, it suddenly struck him: she meant everybody, including the doctors! Nosilewska too? He tried to ask Staszek, as delicately as possible, whether Nosilewska was perhaps a little strange, but his friend snorted.

"Nosilewska?" Staszek launched into a heated defense: "Ridiculous! She comes from the best family." He's hopelessly in love with her, Stefan realized. Staszek suddenly looked different to him. He noticed the badly shaved spot on his bobbing Adam's apple, his ugly teeth, an emerging pimple, the receding hairline where a few years ago there had been lush dark waves.

He doesn't stand a chance, Stefan thought.

Stefan himself had no interest in her. She was beautiful, even very beautiful, with extraordinary eyes, but something about her repelled him.

As they walked, Staszek remembered Sekułowski and decided to introduce Stefan to him.

"A fantastically brilliant man," Staszek explained, "but scatterbrained. You can have a great conversation, but don't set him off. And watch your manners, will you? He's very touchy."

51

"I'll be careful," Stefan promised.

They went outside to get to the recovery wing. The skies were clearing, the wind tearing great holes in the gray, fluffy clouds. Fog wafted low over the trees.

They came across a man in a short coat pushing a wheelbarrow full of dirt. He was a Jew, powerfully built and dark-skinned, with a beard that started almost at his eyes.

"Good morning, sir," he said to Stefan, ignoring Staszek. "Have you forgotten me, doctor? Yes, I see that you don't remember me."

"I'm not sure," Stefan began as he stopped and returned the other man's bow. Staszek stood by in obvious amusement, kicking at a weed with the tip of his shoe.

"Nagiel, Salomon Nagiel. I did your dad's metalwork, don't you remember?"

Something clicked in Stefan's mind. In fact there had been a handyman with whom his father would sometimes disappear into the workshop to build a model.

"Do you know what I do here?" Nagiel continued. "I am the First Angel."

Stefan felt foolish. Nagiel came closer and whispered earnestly, "A week from now there's going to be a big assembly. The Lord God Himself will be there, and David, and all the Prophets and Archangels. Everyone. I have influence there, so if you need anything, doctor, just let me know, and I'll take care of it."

"No, I don't need anything."

Stefan grabbed Staszek by the arm and pulled him toward the door. The Jew stood watching, leaning on his shovel.

"Who knows what laymen think an asylum is," Stefan was saying as they turned into a long corridor with yellow tiles. At a landing another corridor led off to the left, lighted by small, widely spaced lamps that somehow suggested a forest. They moved in and out of darkness as they walked.

52

"The symptoms you've seen so far are pretty typical. Delusions, hallucinations, motor excitement, dementia, catatonia, mania, and so on. But pay attention now."

He stopped under a frosted-glass lamp at an ordinary door with a handle and lock.

They entered a small, airy room with a bed against the wall, a few white chairs, and a table with an orderly stack of thick books on top. Numerous sheets of paper crumpled into balls lay on the floor. A man in violet pajamas with silver stripes sat with his back to the door. When he turned around, Stefan recalled a photograph from an illustrated magazine. He was a tall man, almost handsome, but putting on weight that was obscuring his sharp, regular features. He had prominent eyebrows flecked with gray like his temples, and his eyes looked bright, lively, and strong, capable of staring relentlessly, now vacant with relaxation. They were colorless, and picked up the hues of their surroundings. They were light now. The poet's skin, pale from his confinement indoors, seemed almost transparent; under his eyes it sagged into barely perceptible pockets.

"Allow me to introduce my colleague, Doctor Trzyniecki," Staszek said. "He's come to work with us for a while. An excellent participant in discussions of ideas."

"But only as a dilettante," said Stefan, pleased at Sekułowski's brief, warm handshake. They sat. It might have looked strange: two men in white coats, stethoscopes and hammers sticking indiscreetly out of their pockets, and an older man in wild pajamas.

They chatted about this and that for a while, and then Sekułowski remarked, "Medicine can offer a pretty good window on infinity. Sometimes I regret not having studied it systematically."

"You are speaking with an expert on psychopathology," Staszek said to Stefan, who noted that his friend was more restrained and rigid than usual. He's trying his best, Stefan thought.

Stefan said that no one had yet written a novel about medicine believably depicting the profession.

"A scribbler's job," the poet said, smiling politely but dismissively. "A mirror to everyday life? What does that have to do with literature? By that view, doctor—contrary to what Witkacy says—the novel would be the art form of the peeping Tom."

"I was thinking of the whole complexity of the profession . . . the transformation of a person who enters the halls of the university knowing people only on the outside and . . . comes out a doctor."

He knew that sounded stupid. To his unpleasant surprise, Stefan realized that he was having trouble formulating his thoughts and choosing his words, that he was confused, like a freshman in front of a professor, even though he felt no awe of Sekułowski.

"It seems to me that we have no more knowledge of our bodies than of the most distant star," the poet said quietly.

"But we are discovering the laws that govern the body."

"Not until the majority of biological theses have their antitheses. Scientific theory is intellectual chewing gum."

"But allow me to ask," Stefan replied, slightly impatient. "What did you do when you were sick?"

"I called the doctor." Sekułowski smiled. His smile was as bright as a child's. "But when I was eighteen years old, I realized how many morons became doctors. Since then I have had a panicky fear of illness, because how can you entrust your body to someone more stupid than yourself?"

"Sometimes that's best. Haven't you ever felt like confiding things you would conceal from those closest to you, to the first stranger that comes along?"

"And who, according to you, is close?"

"Well, your parents, for instance."

"Mommy and Daddy know best?" Sekułowski asked. "Parents are supposed to be close? Why not the coelacanth? After all, your biology teaches us that they are the first link in the chain of evolution, so why shouldn't intimacy extend to the whole family, lizards included? Do you know anyone who ever conceived a child with a warm thought to its future intellectual life?"

"Well, what about women?"

"You must be joking. The sexes deal with each other out of complicated motives, probably a consequence of some twisted protein that lacked something here and had something sticking out there, but how do we get from there to closeness? To intellectual closeness. Is your leg close to you?"

"What does my leg have to do with it?" Stefan could see that he wasn't holding up his end; Sekułowski was batting the conversation around like a ball with a racket.

"Everything. Your leg is obviously close, because you can experience it in two ways, with your eyes closed as a 'conscious feeling of possessing a leg,' and when you look at it or touch it—in other words, as an object. Unfortunately, no other human being is ever more than an object."

"That's absurd. Surely you don't mean to say that you've never had a friend, that you've never loved?"

"Now we're getting somewhere!" Sekułowski exclaimed. "Let's assume that I have. But what does that have to do with closeness? No one can be closer to me than I am to myself, and sometimes I am a stranger to myself."

He lowered his eyelids heavily, as if resigning from the world. This conversation was like wandering in a labyrinth. Stefan decided to persevere and do his best. It might be fun.

"But your literature is no bargain. One takes hold of words too one-sidedly and glosses over details . . ."

"Go on," the poet encouraged him.

"A literary work is a matter of conventions, and talent is the ability to break them. I'm not saying it has to be realism. Any literary style can be good, provided the author respects the internal logic of the work. If you have your hero walk through a wall once, you have to let him do it again . . ."

"Excuse me, but what is the purpose of literature, as you see it?" Sekułowski asked softly, as if he were falling asleep.

But Stefan had not finished; the interruption confused him and he lost his train of thought.

"Literature teaches . . ."

"Oh really?" The poet sighed. "And what does Beethoven teach?"

"What does Einstein teach?"

Stefan's impatience now bordered on irritation. Sekułowski definitely had an overblown reputation. Why go easy on him?

The poet smiled quietly, very satisfied. "Nothing, naturally," he said. "He's playing, friend. Except that some people don't know it. Turn on a light every time you give a dog a piece of kielbasa, and after a while the dog will salivate at the sight of the light. Show a man enough ink scrawled on paper, and after a while he'll say it is a model for the universe. It's neurology, obedience school, that's all."

"What's the kielbasa in that example?" Stefan asked quickly, feeling like a fencer scoring a touch. But Sekułowski was not slow with his riposte.

"Einstein, or some other worthy authority, is the kielbasa. Isn't mathematics a form of intellectual tag? And logic, chess played by the strictest rules. It's like that child's game with string, where two players twist it around their fingers in artful combinations, adding more and more twists until they come back to the starting point. Have you ever seen Peano and Russell's proof that two plus two is four? It takes up an entire dense page of algebraic symbols. Everybody is playing, and so am I. Have you seen my play *The Flower Garden*? I call it a chemical drama. The flowers are bacteria, and the garden is the human body in which they multiply. A fierce battle between tuberculosis bacilli and the leukocytes is going on. After seizing the armor of the lipoids, which is a sort of magic cap of invisibility, the bacteria unite under the leadership of the Supermicrobe, defeat the leukocytes, and then, just as a blissful and blessed future is unfolding before them, the garden sinks under them. In other words, the human being dies and the poor little plants have to die along with it."

Stefan did not know the play.

"Forgive me for talking about myself," the poet said. "But each of us, after all, is a kind of blueprint for the world. The trouble is that the plan is not always well executed. An awful lot of bungling goes into the making of human beings. And the world," he said, looking down through the window as if he saw something amusing, "is just a collection of the most fantastic oddities, whose existence no one can explain. The easiest thing, of course, is to make believe you don't see anything, that whatever is, simply is. I do it myself all the time. But it isn't enough. I cannot remember the exact figure—my memory is failing these days—but I once read the odds of one living cell arising out of the multitude of atoms. It was something like one in a trillion. And that those cells should come together in however many billions you need to make up the body of a living human being! Every one of us is a lottery ticket that hit the jackpot: a few dozen years of life, what fun! In a world of superheated gases, nebulae spiraling to whiteness, and the cosmic absolute zero, suddenly a protein pops up, some greasy jelly that immediately tends to decompose into a puff of bacteria and decay. A hundred thousand subterfuges sustain this weird field of energy, which divides matter into order and chaos. A node of space crawls across an empty landscape. And why? Haven't you ever wondered why there are clouds and trees, golden-brown autumn and gray winter, why the scenery changes through the seasons, why the beauty of it all strikes us like a hammer-blow? Why does it happen that way? By rights we should all be black interstellar dust, shreds of the Magellanic Cloud. The normal state of things is the roaring of the stars, showers of meteors, vacuum, darkness, and death."

He leaned back on his pillow exhausted and said in a deep, low voice:

> Only the dead know the tunes
> The live world dances to.

"What does literature mean to you, then?" Stefan dared to ask after a long pause.

"For the reader it is an attempt to escape. For the creator, an attempt at redemption."

"You're a mystic . . ." Stefan was not doing well in this conversation: he couldn't play his best cards, because Seku-łowski would snort and drop down from infinity.

"A mystic? Who told you that? Here in Poland you publish four poems and they pin a little card on you with a label that sticks beyond your death: 'subtle lyricist,' 'stylist,' 'vitalist.' Critics—or critins, as I sometimes call them—are the physicians of literature: they make wrong diagnoses just like you, and in just the same way they know how things ought to be but they can't do anything. So they've mysticized me now, have they? Well, one more weirdness to add to the million others: though possessing brains, they can think with their intestines."

"This conversation is slightly one-sided," Stefan said, deciding to rally his forces for a frontal attack to conquer Seku-łowski. He had completely forgotten about medicine. "Instead of a dialogue you're having a double monologue with yourself. I do know your work. Somewhere you propose the existence of a consciousness different from the 'Consciousness of Being.' You describe the nonexistent worlds of Riemann. But as you say yourself, the world that surrounds us is interesting enough. Why do you write so little about it?"

"The world that surrounds us? Oh, so you think I dream up worlds? But you have no doubt about the identity of the world that surrounds—for example, the one you're sitting at the center of, on that white chair?"

Stefan thought and said, "For the most part, no."

Sekułowski heard only the "no," which was all he needed.

"I see a different world. Recently Doctor Krzeczotek let me look into a microscope. As he later told me, in it he saw pink buffering epithelia, among which appeared, in a palisade configuration, dark diphtherial corynebacteria of the characteristic spadiceous configuration. Do I have it right?"

Staszek nodded.

"I saw an archipelago of brown islands and coral atolls in a sky-blue sea with pink icebergs drifting on a trembling stream."

"Those atolls were the bacteria," Staszek remarked.

"Yes, but I didn't see bacteria. So where is our common world? When you look at a book, do you see the same thing as a bookbinder?"

"So you doubt even the possibility of communication with another person?"

"This discussion is too academic. All I will admit is that I do exaggerate certain lines in my sketch of the world, and that the attempt to be consistent can lead to inconsistency. Nothing more."

"Logical absurdity, in other words? That is a possibility, but I don't know why . . ."

"Each of us is a possibility, one of many, that has emerged

59

from necessity," Sekułowski interrupted, and Stefan recalled an idea that had come to him in solitude one day. He voiced it, thinking it might be impressive.

"Did you ever think, 'I, who was once one sperm and one egg'?"

"That's interesting. Do you mind if I make a note of it? Unless, of course, you're gathering your own literary material?" Sekułowski asked. Stefan said nothing, feeling robbed but unable to make a formal protest. The poet wrote several words in a large, sloping hand on a sheet of paper he took from a book. The book was Joyce's *Ulysses*.

"You have been speaking, gentlemen, about consistency and its consequence," said Staszek, who had been silent until now. "What do you have to say about the Germans? The consequence of their ideology would be the biological annihilation of our nation."

"Politicians are too stupid for us to be able to predict their actions through reason," answered Sekułowski as he carefully replaced the cap of his green and amber Pelikan pen. "But in this case your hypothesis cannot be ruled out."

"What should be done, then?"

"Play the flute, collect butterflies," retorted Sekułowski, who now seemed bored with the conversation. "We achieve our freedom in various ways. Some do it at the expense of others, which is ugly, but effective. Others try to find cracks in the situation through which they can escape. We should not be afraid of the word 'madness.' Let me tell you that I can perform acts that seem mad in order to manifest my freedom."

"Such as?" asked Stefan, although he thought that Staszek, whom he glimpsed out of the corner of his eye, was making some sort of warning gesture.

"For example," said Sekułowski amiably, at which he wrinkled his face, opened his eyes wide, and bellowed through distended lips like a cow. Stefan turned red. Staszek glanced off to the side with a grimace that bore the hint of a smile.

"Quod erat demonstrandum," said the poet. "I was too lazy to resort to something more eloquent."

Stefan suddenly regretted his effort. Why cast these pearls before swine?

"This has nothing to do with genuine madness," Sekułowski said. "It was only a small demonstration. We should expand our potential, and not only toward the normal. We should also look for ways out of the situation that others don't notice."

"How about in front of a firing squad?" Stefan asked drily, but with inward passion.

"There it may be possible to distinguish oneself from the animals in the manner of meeting death. What would you do in such a situation, doctor?"

"Well, I'd . . ." Stefan did not know what to say. Until then he felt that the words had been sliding off his tongue automatically, but now an emptiness filled his mouth. After a long pause he croaked, "It seems to me that we are marginal. This whole hospital—it isn't a typical phenomenon. The atypical made typical." His formulation cheered him. "The Germans, the war, the defeat, here it's all felt very indirectly. At most, as a distant echo."

"A yard full of wrecks, is that it? While undamaged ships sail the seas," said Sekułowski, looking up at the ceiling. "You, gentlemen, try to mend the works of the Creator, who has botched more than one immortal soul."

He got up from the bed and paced the room, loudly clearing his throat several times as though tuning his voice.

"Is there anything else I can demonstrate for you, gracious audience?" he asked, standing in the center of the room with his arms crossed. His face lit up. "It's coming," he whispered. He leaned forward slightly, looking up so intently that they all froze, drawn into a vortex of strange anticipation. When the tension became unbearable, the poet began to speak:

> Place gently on my grave a ribboned spray
> Of pearly worms. Let those worms crawl
> Through my skull, a decaying ballet
> Of ptomaine, raw flesh whitening, that's all.

Then he bowed and turned toward the window, as if he could no longer see them.

"I thought I told you . . ." Staszek began as soon as they left.

"I didn't do anything."

"You provoked him. You have to speak to him gently, and you put the pedal to the floor right away. You were more concerned with being right than with listening to him."

"Did you like that poem?"

"In spite of everything, I have to say I did. God knows how much abnormality there is in genius sometimes, and vice versa."

"So. Sekułowski the genius!" said Stefan, his feelings hurt as if he were the one being judged.

"I'll give you his book. You haven't read *Blood without a Face*, have you?"

"No."

"It'll knock you out."

At that Staszek left Stefan, who realized that he was standing in front of his own door. He went inside to look for some piramidon in his drawer. He had a pounding headache.

During evening rounds, Stefan tried in vain to avoid the withered blonde. She pounced on him. He took her to Nosilewska's office.

"Doctor, I want to tell you everything from the beginning,"

she said, nervously wringing her emaciated fingers. "I was caught with lard on me. So I acted mad, because I was afraid they'd send me to a camp. But this is worse than a camp. I'm afraid of all these lunatics."

Stefan asked her a series of questions.

"What's your name?

"What's the difference between a priest and a nun?

"What are windows for?

"What do you do in church?"

Her answers suggested that she was indeed completely normal.

"How did you manage to convince them?"

"Well, I have a sister-in-law at John the Divine's, and I saw and heard. I pretend to talk to somebody who's not there, I pretend to see him, and then the fun starts."

"What am I supposed to do with you?"

"Let me out of here." She reached out her hands to him.

"It's not that simple, my dear lady. You'll have to spend some time under observation."

"How much time, doctor? Oh, why did I do it?"

"You wouldn't be any better off in a camp."

"But I can't stand being with that woman who messes herself, doctor. Please. My husband will show his gratitude."

"None of that," Stefan said with professional indignation. Now he had hit upon the right tone. "I'll have you transferred to the other room, where they're more peaceful. You can go now."

"It doesn't even matter anymore now. They squeal and scream and sing and roll their eyes, and I'm afraid I'll go crazy too."

Over the next few days, Stefan got the hang of how to write a case history without thinking about it, stringing a few hackneyed phrases together. Almost everyone else did the same.

He also figured Rygier out. The psychiatrist was undoubtedly an educated man, but his intelligence was like a Japanese garden: make-believe bridges and paths, very beautiful but quite narrow and purposeless. His understanding ran in grooves. The elements of his knowledge were cemented to each other so that he could use them only as if they were entries in a textbook.

After a week, Stefan no longer found the ward so revolting. Poor women, he thought, but some of them, especially the maniacs, prided themselves on a familiarity with the saints that went beyond the intent of church dogma.

Pajączkowski's nameday fell on Sunday. The boss appeared in a freshly pressed coat, his sparse beard carefully combed. He blinked placidly behind his glasses like an old bird, as a woman schizophrenic from the convalescent wing recited a poem in his honor. Then an alcoholic sang. Last but not least was a choir of psychopaths, but they ruined the festivities by grabbing the old man and tossing him up toward the ceiling, above a net of upraised hands. With some effort, the old man was rescued from the patients. The doctors then formed up into a procession as in a cloister—the abbot at the front, the brothers behind—and went into the men's ward, where a hypochondriac who was sure he had cancer made a speech, interrupted by three paralytics who suddenly broke into song— "The poor man died in an army hospital"—and could not be convinced to stop. Later there was a modest meal in the attic of the doctors' building, and Pajpak tried to conclude the evening with a patriotic speech. It did not come off. The little old man's head started trembling, he cried into his glass, spilled cumin-flavored vodka all over the table, and finally, to everyone's relief, sat down.

Doctor Angelicus

Webs of intrigue were spread through the hospital, discreetly awaiting any newcomer's first misstep. Someone was trying to oust Pajączkowski, weaving rumors about an imminent change of directors, rejoicing in every conflict, but Stefan observed this landscape of dwarfed personalities like someone staring into an aquarium, interested but detached.

He was drawn to the company of Sekułowski. They always parted amiably, but it annoyed Stefan that the poet felt so at home in his world of phantoms. Sekułowski treated him as no more than a sparring partner, regarding his own mind as the measure of all things.

Reports of mass arrests in Warsaw came in. There were rumors of the hurried creation of ghettos. Filtered through the hospital walls, however, such stories sounded misty and implausible. Many veterans of the September campaign who had temporarily lost their mental bearings during the fighting were now leaving the asylum. This made things slightly roomier; in some of the wards patients had been sleeping two and three to a bed.

But problems with provisions—especially medicines—were

growing. Pajpak considered the problem carefully and then issued the most far-reaching measures of economy. Scopolamine, morphine, barbiturates, and even bromine were placed under lock and key. Insulin, which had been used for shock therapy, was replaced by cardiazol, and what was left of that was doled out sparingly. Statistics were vague. No clear trend in the census of the community of the mad had yet emerged from the oscillating figures. Numbers in some classifications shrank, others stagnated or rose. It was a time of indecision.

April arrived. Days of bright rain and greenery were interrupted by snowy spells that seemed to have been borrowed from December. Stefan woke early one Sunday with an emphatic sun dyeing his dreams purple through his eyelids. He looked out the window. The view was like a great painter's sketch with a broad brush, and new variations of the same sketch followed, each containing fresh color and detail. Fleece-like fog crept through the long valley between ridges like the backs of sleeping animals, and black brushstrokes of branches were covered in the swell. Dark irregular shapes showed through the fog here and there, as if the brush had slipped. Then a trace of gold filtered into the white from above, there was an unsettled moment when white spirals appeared and drifted out to become a cloud on the horizon that soon thinned and receded until day shined through as pure as a bare chestnut.

Stefan went out for a walk. He left the road. Every scrap of ground was covered with green: it seethed in the ditches and spurted from beneath stones; blossoms were bursting, covering the distant trees in delicate celadon clouds. Exposed to the warm breeze, he tramped up a hill and reached its ridge through last year's dry, rustling grass. The fields lay below like slightly soiled stripes in a peasant costume. Water droplets, blue and white, shimmered on every stalk, each one holding fragments of the image of the world. The distant forest angled toward the horizon like an underwater silver sculpture. The tops of trees on the slope below stood out against the sky, brown constellations of sticky buds. He walked in their direction. A mass of bushes blocked his way, and as he detoured around it, he heard heavy breathing.

He drew close to an entangled thicket. Sekułowski was kneeling inside it. Stefan could barely hear his laugh, but it made his skin crawl.

"Come here, doctor," the poet said without looking up.

Stefan pushed through the branches. In the middle was a circular clearing. Sekułowski was looking at a small mound of earth where thin files of ants moved around a reddish earthworm.

Stefan said nothing. Sekułowski looked him up and down, then stood up and commented, "This is only a model."

He took Stefan by the arm and led him out of the thicket. The hospital was gray and small in the distance. The surgical wing shined like a child's red block that had been dropped. Sekułowski sat in the grass and began to scribble rapidly in a notebook.

"Do you like to watch ants?" Stefan asked.

"I don't like it, but sometimes I have to. Were it not for us, insects would be the most horrifying thing in nature. Because life is the opposite of mechanism, and mechanism the opposite of life. But insects are living mechanisms, a mockery, nature's joke. Midges, caterpillars, beetles—we should tremble before them. Dread, the greatest dread."

He bent his head and went on writing. Stefan looked over his shoulder and read out the last words: ". . . the world—battle between God and nothingness."

He asked if it was going to be a poem.

"How should I know?"

"Who would know if not you?"

"And you want to be a psychiatrist?"

"Poetry takes a stand about two worlds: the one we can see and the one we have lived through," Stefan began hesitantly. "Mickiewicz wrote, 'Our nation, like lava . . .' "

"This is not a classroom," Sekułowski interrupted in a murmur. "Mickiewicz could say what he wanted because he was a romantic, but our nation is like cow flop: dry on the outside and you know what on the inside. And not just ours, either. But please don't talk to me about taking a stand, because it makes me sick."

He surveyed the sunlit scene for a while.

"What is a poem, then?"

Sekułowski sighed.

"I see a poem as a multicolored strip behind peeling plaster, in separate, shining fragments. I try to connect hands and horizons, glances and the objects imprisoned in them. That's how it is in daylight. At night—because sometimes it happens at night—poems are like spiraling curves that grow to completeness by themselves. The hardest thing is to hold onto them through waking into consciousness."

"That poem you recited the first time we met, was it day or night?"

"That was a day poem."

Stefan tried to praise it, but was rebuffed sharply.

"Nonsense. You don't understand at all. What do you know about poetry anyway? Writing is a damnable compulsion. Someone who can stand and watch the person he loves most die and, without wanting to, pick out everything worth describing to the last convulsion, that's a real writer. A philistine would protest: how awful! But it's not awful, it's just suffering. It's not a career, not something you pick like a desk job. The only writers who have any peace are the ones who don't write.

68

And there are some like that. They wallow in a sea of possibilities. To express a thought, you first have to limit it, and that means kill it. Every word I speak robs me of a thousand others, and every line I write means giving up another. I have to create an artificial certainty. When those flakes of plaster fall away, I sense that deep down, behind the golden fragments, lies an unspeakable abyss. It's there, for sure, but every attempt to reach it ends in failure. And my terror . . ."

He fell silent and took a deep breath.

"Every word I feel is the last. That I won't be able to go on. Of course you don't understand. You can't. The fear—how can I explain it? Because words pour out of me like water coming under a door in a flood. I don't know what's behind the door. I don't know if it's the last wave. I can't control the force of the flow. And you want me to take a stand. I can be free only through the people I write about, but that too is illusion.

"Who am I writing for? The days of the caveman are past. He ate the hot brains out of his friends' skulls, and used his blood to draw works of art on the cave walls that have not been equaled since. The renaissance is gone, with its geniuses and heretics sizzling at the stake. The hordes who learned to ride the seas and winds have come and gone. Now we are in the era of dwarves quartered in barracks, music in tin cans, and helmets under which you cannot see the stars. Then, they say, equality and brotherhood will come. Why equality, why freedom, when lack of equality gives birth to visionary scenes and fires of despair, when danger can squeeze something out of man worth more than well-tended surfeit. I don't want to give up these colossal differences, these tensions. If it was up to me, I would keep the palaces and the slums, and the fortresses!"

"Someone once told me," Stefan said, "the story of a Russian prince of very tender spirit. He had a beautiful view from the window of his palace on a hill overlooking the village. But a few thatch-roofed cottages were in the way, so he ordered them burned down, and the charred rafters that remained provided just the touch he had been looking for."

"Don't blame me," Sekułowski said. "Are we supposed to work for the masses? I'm not Mephisto, doctor, but I like to think things through. Philanthropy? Tutored virgins with dried-up hormones are condemned to do good works, and if you want to talk about the theory of revolution, beggars don't have time for it. That is the vocation of well-fed rebels. It's always bad for the people. Anyone who wants peace, quiet, and comfort will find it in the grave, but not in this life. But why be so abstract? I myself grew up in poverty, doctor, that you could not imagine. I had my first job when I was three months old, you know? My mother lent me to a beggar woman who thought she could do better with a baby in her arms. When I was eight, I used to hang around in front of a nightclub, and when the elegant crowd came out, I would pick the most beautifully dressed couple and follow right behind them, spitting on their sealskins and beavers and muskrats, spitting as hard as I could on those perfumed furs and on those women until my mouth went dry. What I've got now, I fought for. People with real ability always make it."

"And geniuses are supposed to regard everybody else as fertilizer?"

Stefan sometimes thought that way himself. He might have been talking to himself. He had forgotten that when the poet was irritated, he could be abusive.

"Ah, yes," Sekułowski said, leaning back on his elbows and looking up at the flaring clouds with a contemptuous smile. "Would you rather be fertilizer for future generations? Lay your bones at the altar? Leave me alone, doctor. The one thing I can't stand is boredom."

70

Stefan's feelings were hurt. "And what about the mass arrests in Warsaw and the deportations to Germany? Doesn't that bother you? Are you going back there when you leave here?"

"Why should the arrests bother me any more than the Tartar invasions of the thirteenth century? Because of the accidental coincidence of time?"

"Don't argue with history. History is always right. You can't hide your head in the sand."

"History will win. Survival of the fittest," said the poet. "It's true that even though I'm a world unto myself, I'm just a speck of dust in the avalanche of events. But nothing will ever force me to think like a speck of dust!"

"Do you know that the Germans are talking about liquidating the mentally ill?"

"They say there are about twenty million lunatics in the world. What they need is a slogan that can unite them—there's going to be a holy war," Sekułowski said, lying down on his back. The sun shined more brightly. Sensing that the poet was trying to escape, Stefan decided to pin him down. "I don't understand you. The first time we talked you spoke of the art of dying."

"I don't see any contradiction," Sekułowski said, his good mood obviously gone. "I don't care about the state's independence. The important thing is internal independence."

"So you think the fate of other people . . ."

Sekułowski interrupted, his face trembling. "Pig," he shouted. "Idiot!"

He suddenly ran off, loping down the hillside. Confused, the blood rushing to his face, Stefan ran after him. The poet pulled away and yelled, "Clown!"

By the time they got to the asylum, Sekułowski had calmed down. Looking at the wall, he remarked, "Doctor, you are ill-bred. I would even go so far as to say that you're vulgar, since you try to offend me whenever we talk."

Stefan was furious, but acted the doctor forgiving a patient's outburst.

Three weeks later, Stefan was transferred to Kauters's division. Before starting work he called on his new superior. The surgeon came to the door wearing a loose-fitting dark blue smoking jacket with silver stripes. As they walked down the long dark hallway to the apartment, Stefan explained his visit, but then he fell silent, stunned.

His first impression was of brown punctuated with black and throbbing violet. Something vaguely resembling a rosary of pale shells hung from the ceiling, and the floor was covered with a black and orange oriental carpet depicting gondolas, flames, or salamanders. The walls were covered with engravings, pictures in black frames, and a narrow glass cabinet on legs of buffalo horns. A crocodile's snout with bared teeth hung on the wall above a Venus flytrap. A low octagonal glass table was inlaid with garish amber flowers. Bookcases on either side of the door were carelessly strewn with leather-bound books and moldy incunabula with yellowed pages. Enormous atlases and gray albums with blood-red and multicolored spines stuck out among the trinkets lining the edges of the shelves.

Kauters seated his guest, who could not take his eyes off the Japanese woodcuts, ancient Indian figurines, and gaudy porcelain baubles. The surgeon said he was glad Stefan had come and asked him to tell him something about himself. Stefan found it hard to answer such an insipid request with anything intelligent. Kauters asked if he planned to specialize.

Stefan half muttered something, enjoying the touch of the raw silk cover on the arm of the chair, a colossus upholstered in rich leather. Gradually he began to get his bearings: near the window was the working area of the room. Reproductions and plaster masks hung above the large desk. He recognized some of them. There was the iconography of the cretin: a flabby, snail-like body with no neck and a bug-eyed face, a worm-like tongue peeking out of the half-open mouth. Several of Leonardo's hideous faces were framed in glass. One of them, with a chin protruding like the toe of an old shoe and with nests of wrinkles for eye sockets, seemed to stare at Stefan. There were distorted skulls and Goya's monster with ears like folded bat wings and a clenched, twisted jaw. Between the windows hung a large alabaster mask from the church of Santa Maria Formosa: on the right side the face looked like a leering drunk, while the left half was a swollen mess with a bulging eye and a few shovel-shaped teeth.

Noting Stefan's interest, Kauters began showing him around with evident satisfaction. He was a passionate collector. He had an oversized album of Meunier prints illustrating early devices for treating the deranged: great wooden drums, ingenious torturous leg-irons that were said to do wonders for the beclouded mind, and a pear-shaped iron gag secured by chains to prevent the patient from screaming.

Returning to his chair, Stefan noticed a row of tall jars on top of a cabinet. Murky purple and blue shapes floated in them.

"Ah, my display set," said Kauters, pointing to them with a black cane. "This is a cephalothoracopagus, and a craniopagus parietalis, a beautiful example that, and a rare epigastrium. This last embryo is a perfect diprosopus; there's a kind of leg growing out of the palate, slightly damaged during delivery, I'm afraid. There are a few others too, but not as interesting."

He excused himself and opened the door. Mrs. Kauters came

73

in carrying a black lacquered tray with a steaming poppy-colored china coffee service with silver rims. Stefan was astounded again.

Amelia Kauters had a large, soft mouth and austere eyes not unlike her husband's. She smiled, showing convex, slightly dull teeth. You could not call her beautiful, but she was definitely striking. Her black hair was in heavy braids that swung when she moved. Aware that she had beautiful shoulders, she wore a sleeveless blouse with an amethyst triangle pin at the neck.

"How do you like our figurines?" the surgeon asked, offering Stefan a sugarbowl shaped like a Viking ship. "Well, people who have given up as much as we have are entitled to originality."

"It's a comfortably padded nest," Amelia said, petting a fluffy cat that had climbed noiselessly into her lap. The full, languid lines of her thighs disappeared into the black folds of her dress.

Stefan was no longer stunned. He took it all in. The coffee was superb, the best-tasting he had had in years. Some of the furniture looked like what a Hollywood director might use for the "salon of a Hungarian prince"—if he knew nothing about Hungary. The doors of Kauters's apartment were like a knife cutting off the ubiquitous hospital atmosphere of spotless white walls and shiny radiators.

Looking at the surgeon's sallow face, his eyelids fluttering behind his glasses like impatient butterflies, Stefan decided that the room had to represent its owner's mind. That's what he was thinking when Sekułowski's name came up.

"Sekułowski?" The surgeon shrugged. "You mean Sekuła."

"He changed his name?"

"No, why should he? He took a pseudonym—what was that book called?" he asked, turning to his wife.

74

Amelia Kauters smiled. *"Reflections on Statebuilding.* Haven't you read it, doctor? No? Well, we don't have a copy. There was such a furor. How can I describe it? Well, it was a sort of essay. Supposedly about everything, but mainly about communism. The left attacked him, which was good publicity. He got very popular."

Stefan was examining his fingernails.

"But I don't remember it myself," Amelia Kauters suddenly said. "After all, I was just a child. I heard about it later. I like his poetry."

She got up to show Stefan a book of poems. As she did so, she knocked over another book, thin, in a soft pale binding. Stefan bent over to pick it up, and as he did Kauters pointed at it. "Beautiful binding, isn't it? Skin from the inside of a woman's thigh."

Stefan pulled his hand away, and the surgeon took the book from him.

"My husband has a funny sense of humor," Amelia Kauters said. "But it's so soft. Look. Touch it." As she spoke in her low voice, she delicately raised her hand and touched the corners of her mouth and eyes with nimble, furtive movements.

Stefan mumbled something and went back to his chair, sweating.

He felt that this strange scene was a microcosm of the people locked up in the wards. Peculiarity flourished in human beings who were removed from the usual city soil, like mutated flowers grown in special greenhouses. Then he changed his mind. Perhaps Kauters had shunned the city and created this dusky, violet interior because he was different to begin with.

On his way out, Stefan noticed an aquarium full of reflected rainbows standing behind a small screen. A goldfish floated belly-up on the surface. The image stayed with him, and he felt as if he had just completed some taxing intellectual task.

He did not feel like going straight to supper, but was afraid someone might notice his absence, so he forced himself. No-silewska sat there as always, somnolent, polite, occasionally flashing that priceless smile. Staszek—the fool—devoured her with his eyes, thinking that no one noticed.

That night Stefan could not fall asleep and finally took luminal. He dreamed of Mrs. Kauters carrying a basket of headless fish. She kept trying to give it to him. He woke up with his heart pounding and could not get to sleep until morning.

Sekułowski, it turned out, was not at all offended. He told Staszek to ask Stefan to drop in sometime before noon. Stefan went right after breakfast. The writer was sitting at the window looking at a large photograph showing a ballroom full of amused, relaxed people.

"Look at these faces," he said. "Typical Americans. Look how self-satisfied they are, their lives all worked out: lunch, dinner, bed, and subway. No time for metaphysics, for contemplating the brutality of Things. Truly, the Old World has a special destiny: we must choose between less or more noble varieties of suffering."

Stefan talked about his visit to Kauters. He realized that by discussing a colleague with Sekułowski he was violating an unwritten law, but he had a justification: he and the poet were both above such conventions. But of course he did not mention what Kauters had said about Sekułowski.

"Don't be upset," the poet said affably. "What is hideousness, after all? In art something can be well or poorly done, no more. Van Gogh paints a couple of old chamberpots and you feel like falling to your knees in awe, while some amateur makes the most beautiful woman look trite. What does it all come down to, anyway? The flash of the world, Glory, catharsis, that's all."

76

But Stefan thought that living in that kind of museum was too strange.

"You don't like it? You could be wrong. Would you close the window for me, please?" asked the poet.

He looked especially pale in the strong light. The breeze carried the fragrance of magnolia blossoms.

"Remember," Sekułowski went on, "that everything contains everything else. The most distant star swims at the rim of a chalice. Today's morning dew contains last night's mist. Everything is woven into a universal interdependence. No one thing can elude the power of others. Least of all man, the thinking thing. Stones and faces echo in your dreams. The smell of flowers bends the pathways of our thoughts. So why not freely shape that which has an accidental form? Surrounding yourself with gold and ivory trinkets can be like charging a battery. A statue the size of your finger is the expression of the artist's fantasy, distilled over the years. And those hundreds of hours are not futile—we can warm ourselves in front of a statue as though it were a fire."

He stopped and added with a sigh, "Sometimes I am happy gazing at a stone . . . that's not me, that's Chang Kiu-Lin. A great poet."

"How early?"

"Eighth century."

"You said, 'the thinking thing.' You're a materialist, aren't you?" Stefan asked.

"A materialist? Oh yes, the magic wand of classification. I think that man and the world are made of the same substance, but I don't know what that substance is—it is beyond the reach of words. But they are two arches that hold each other up. Neither can stand alone. I can tell you that the table over there will continue to exist after our death. But for whom? For the flies? It cannot be 'our table,' and there is no such thing as 'being' in general. The object immediately disintegrates. Without people, what is the table? A varnished board on four legs? A mass of mummified tree cells? A chemical conglomeration of celluloid chains? A whirlpool of electron clouds? No, it must always be something for somebody. That tree outside the window exists for me, and also for the microbes that feed on its sap. For me it is a fragment of forest, a branch against the sky. For them, a single leaf is a green ocean, and a branch an entire universe. Do we—the microbe and I—share a common tree? Not at all. So what makes our point of view any better than the microbe's?"

"But we are not microbes," said Stefan.

"Not yet, but we will be. We will become nitrogenous bacteria in the soil, we will enter the roots of trees, become part of an apple that someone will eat while philosophizing, just as we are philosophizing now, and while enjoying the sight of rosy clouds that contain the water of our former bodies. And so on, in an endless circle. The number of permutations is infinite."

Satisfied, Sekułowski lit a cigarette.

"So you're an atheist?" Stefan asked.

"Yes, but I do have a small chapel."

"A chapel?"

"Have you read 'A Litany to My Body'?"

Indeed, Stefan remembered that hymn to the lungs, liver, and kidneys. "An original essay."

"No, it's a poem. I keep my philosophical views and my creative work strictly separate, and I forbid anyone to judge me on what I have already written," Sekułowski announced with sudden obstinacy. Dropping his cigarette on the floor, he went on, "But I do pray sometimes. My prayer used to be, 'O God, Who art not.' That once sounded all right. But lately it's the Blind Powers."

78

"What do you mean?"

"I pray to the Blind Powers. Because it is they who rule our bodies, the world, and even the words I am speaking right now. I know they don't listen to prayers," he said, smiling, "but it can't hurt."

It was almost eleven o'clock. Stefan had to start his rounds.

For several weeks Father Niezgłoba, a short, gaunt man with bluish veins along his arms had been in Room 8. He looked as if he had once been a laborer.

"How are you, Father?" Stefan asked softly as he came in.

The priest had been allowed to retain his cassock, which made an irregular dark blot against the white hospital walls. Stefan wanted to be delicate, because he knew that Marglewski, the thin doctor who was in charge of the ward, sometimes called the priest "the ambassador of the kingdom of heaven" and treated him to anecdotes from the lives of church dignitaries. The doctor had considerable knowledge of the subject.

"It's torture, doctor."

The priest's voice was pleasant, though perhaps a bit too soft. He suffered from hallucinations of unchanging content: at a baptismal party, he heard a woman's voice behind him. But when he turned, the voice seemed to come from a place his eye could not see.

"Is the Arabian princess still with you?"

"Yes."

"You realize that it's only a vision, Father, a hallucination?"

The priest shrugged. His eyes were heavy with sleeplessness, tiny lines covering his lids.

"This conversation with you, doctor, might be equally unreal. I hear that voice as clearly as I hear yours."

"Well, don't worry. It'll pass. But no more alcohol ever again."

"I would never have done that," he said with remorse, looking down at the floor. "But my parishioners are such terrible sinners." He sighed. "They were always offended, angry, and persistent, so I . . ."

Stefan checked the man's reflexes mechanically, put the hammer back in his smock, and asked just before he left, "What do you do all day, Father? You must be climbing the walls. Do you want a book?"

"I have a book."

And indeed he took out a dog-eared tome with a black cover.

"Really? What is it?"

"I'm praying."

Stefan suddenly remembered the Blind Powers and stood in the door for a moment. Then, perhaps too abruptly, he left.

He no longer visited Nosilewska's ward. He had lost interest in the fates of the individual patients, as he had in the gruesome pictures in Uncle Ksawery's anatomical atlas, which had fascinated him as a child. He exchanged a few words with Pajpak now and then, and occasionally assisted him on morning rounds.

Working with Kauters, he became acquainted with a ward nurse named Gonzaga. Big-boned and fat, she looked threatening in her wide skirts. But the threat was only potential, for no one had ever seen her angry. She affected people as a scarecrow did sparrows. Her cheeks dropped in heavy folds to the blue line of her mouth. Her enormous hands always held the key in its leather ring, a clipboard of medical records, or a pack of compresses. She never dealt with trays of syringes: there were orderlies for that. Handy with instruments, quiet and solitary, she seemed to have no private life. Kauters appeared to respect her. Once Stefan saw the tall surgeon standing in front of her with both hands on his chest, his shoulders

80

moving nervously, as if he were trying to justify himself, convince her of something, or ask a favor. Sister Gonzaga stood there large and immobile, unblinking, the light from the window falling across her face. The scene was so unusual that it stuck in Stefan's mind. He never found out what it was about. Sister Gonzaga could be found in the corridor at any time of day or night, moving like the moon with even steps invisible under her skirt, her lace cap brightening the dim hallway.

Stefan spoke to her only when ordering procedures or medication for the patients. Once, when he had just come back from seeing Sekułowski and was looking for a bottle in the supply-room cabinet, Sister Gonzaga, who was jotting something down in a notebook, suddenly said, "Sekułowski is worse than a madman. He's a comedian."

Stefan turned around. "Were you speaking to me, Sister?"

"No. I was speaking in general," she replied, and said no more.

Stefan did not recount the incident, but he did ask the poet whether he knew Sister Gonzaga. Sekułowski, however, took no interest in the auxiliary personnel, though he did have a succinct opinion of Kauters: "Have you noticed what a stage decorator's mentality he has?"

"How do you mean?"

"Two-dimensional."

In a far corner of the grounds stood the neglected, nearly forgotten ward for catatonics, overgrown with morning glories that had not yet sprouted leaves. Stefan seldom went there. At first he had yearned to clean out those Augean stables—a gloomy hall with an oppressive blue ceiling in which the patients stood, lay, or knelt in frozen positions. But his reforming impulse had faded quickly.

The catatonics lay on bedframes without mattresses. Their

bodies, caked with dirt, were covered with sores caused by the wires and springs of the bedding. Piercing smells of ammonia and excrement filled the air. This lowest circle of hell, as Stefan called it, rarely saw a nurse. Some unknown force seemed to sustain the existence of these mindless people.

Two young boys attracted Stefan's attention. A Jew from a small town, who had a round head capped with dry, red hair, sat endlessly in his cubicle, bent over on the bed, always naked, with a blanket pulled up over his head. All day long, tirelessly, he called out two words of gibberish. Whenever anyone approached, he raised his voice to a prayerful complaint and shivered. His blue eyes stared permanently at the iron bedframe. The other boy, whose hair was the color of rye, walked up and down the passageway between the main hall and the Jew's cubicle, from the bed in the corner to the wall and back again. In this eight-step Golgotha he always banged against the bed rail, but he was unaware of it. A discolored sore swelled above his hip. He held his hands crossed on his chest or over his face, but he never stopped walking. When someone came in, he would utter a childlike moan that sounded strange coming from a man. And he was becoming a man. Freed of the rule of the intellect, his body led an independent existence, and the arcs of muscle on his slender, statuesque torso shined under his open shirt. His face was as pale as the wall he bounced off, his blue eyes set in an alternating expression of curiosity and entreaty.

Once Stefan went to the catatonics' ward at an unusual hour, after dinner, to check on a suspicion that an orderly named Ewa was doing something improper with the boys, who were always highly agitated after she had been there. The Jew would tremble so violently that the bedframe shook, and the thin boy raced down the narrow corridor, hitting his hip on the bed, bouncing off, and smacking into the wall.

82

The room was filled with misty twilight. The wind rattled a branch against the windowpane. Stefan stopped in the corridor: Nosilewska was standing at the Jew's bed, slowly pulling the blanket off his head. For a moment he tried to resist, tugging with his thick fingers. With an infinitely light and gentle hand, she stroked his stiff, bristly hair. Her face was turned to the window, and she seemed to be looking far off into the distance, but the irregular cracks of the outside wall were only four feet beyond the windowpane.

Stefan looked off to the side; in a patch of shadow he saw the other boy, who, having interrupted his endless journey, was pressed into the embrasure, staring at the woman's silhouette outlined against the window. Stefan wanted to go in and ask for an explanation, but he withdrew and left as quietly as he had come.

Advocatus Diaboli

It was May. The bas-relief crescent of woods that ringed the asylum glistened with generous green. New flowers blossomed every night, and leaves that had hung with folded wings opened to the air. No longer gentle silver columns, the birch trees were loud white flames. The heart-shaped leaves of the poplars drank in the sun's warmth and absorbed its bright hues. Bare mounds of loam showed like honeycombs scattered on the joyous landscape.

Kauters ordered Stefan to examine an engineer named Rabiewski, who had been brought by car from the nearby town. The patient's wife recounted the strange transformation of her husband in recent months. He had been a skilled worker, but after the Germans came and bombed the factory, he began supporting himself by teaching vocational courses. Easygoing and phlegmatic, he had been a passionate fisherman, book collector, and vegetarian. An honest man, he would not hurt a fly. Since the beginning of the year, he had been sleeping more and more. By now it had got so, he would doze off during dinner and wake up with a start like a beetle that had been poked. He became lazy and reluctant to go to his lectures, and at home he was a different man; he would fly into a rage for no reason at all and then quiet down equally suddenly. He would fall asleep for hours and wake up with a throbbing headache. He also began to tell strange jokes—he would burst out laughing at things no one else found funny.

The orderly, a strapping young man known as Young Joseph, to distinguish him from the orderly Joseph, had deft hands that could break the most despairing clinch; he led Rabiewski into the examining room. The patient was a fat, balding man with a wreath of gray hair. He wore a purple hospital robe as he limped to a chair and dropped into it so awkwardly that his teeth snapped together. He answered questions only after a long pause, or after they had been rephrased in the simplest possible terms. At one point he noticed the stethoscope lying on the desk and began to giggle.

Having scrupulously recorded the history of the illness, Stefan began to test the engineer's reflexes. He had him lie down on the oilcloth-covered examining table. The day was bright with sunshine, and reflected prisms showered from all the chrome fittings in the room. While Stefan was tapping the patient's tendons, Kauters appeared.

"Well, how does it look?" he asked, brisk and animated. He listened to Stefan's exposition with satisfaction.

"Interesting," the surgeon said. "For the moment let's put: *suspectio quoad tumorem*. We'll do a specular eye examination. And a tap. And then . . ."

He took the hammer and struck Rabiewski's thin leg.

"Aha! What's this? Please touch your right knee with your left heel. No, not like that. Show him," he told Stefan, and walked over to the window. Stefan explained. Kauters came back with a leaf he had torn from a branch near the window, rubbing it between his fingers. Sniffing his slender, sinewy hand, he said with content, "Perfect. Ataxia too."

85

"Cerebellar, doctor?"

"Perhaps not. Too early to tell. But there is a disturbance in thinking. Abulia. Now let's see." He tore a sheet of paper from his notebook and drew a circle on it. Then he showed it to Rabiewski. "What's this?"

"It's a part," the engineer answered after long thought. His voice sounded pained.

"A part of what?"

"A spiral."

"You see!"

Stefan reported the incident with the stethoscope.

Kauters rubbed his hands. "Perfect. Witzelsucht. A textbook case, don't you think? I'm convinced it's a small tumor in the frontal lobe. Time will tell. Please write everything down."

The patient was lying on the table, his slightly goggled eyes staring at the ceiling. As he exhaled noisily, his lips parted to reveal long, yellow teeth.

That evening, Stefan came down with a headache and fever. He took two aspirin, and Staszek brought a bottle of vodka, which should have helped. But the weakness, chills, and fever lasted for four days. On the fifth day Stefan was finally able to get out of bed. After breakfast he went straight to Rabiewski's room, curious to find out what was happening. The ordinary hospital bed had been replaced by a special one with nets at the sides and on top. The engineer lay as if caught in a web in the cage that they created, no more than a foot and a half high. His whole body seemed swollen. Kauters was leaning over looking at him attentively, moving his head out of the way when the prisoner tried to spit in his face. The thick lines around Rabiewski's mouth were white with foam. The surgeon took off his glasses and Stefan had his first clear look at his eyes. They bulged, devoid of any sparkle, and were dark like the eyes of an insect seen through a magnifying glass.

"The tumor is growing," Stefan said in a half-whisper. The

86

surgeon paid no attention. He backed away again when the patient managed to turn his head and sprayed saliva. The patient grunted, tensing the muscles of his immobilized body.

"Pressure on the motor region," Kauters murmured.

"Are you thinking of operating, doctor?"

"We'll do a tap today."

That evening, the brain that was lashing Rabiewski's body seemed to reach a paroxysm of vexation. Knots of muscles cramped and rippled beneath his sweaty skin. The netting on the bed resonated like strings on a musical instrument. Stefan gave him two injections, which did not help much: the chloral narcosis stilled the fury only for a short while. When he came out of the anesthesia, the engineer reacted to the first light he had seen in many hours and mumbled hoarsely, "I know . . . it's me . . . help."

Stefan shivered. After the tapping of spinal fluid, there was an insignificant improvement. Kauters sat in the room for days on end, pretending that he had just come in to check when Stefan happened to appear. At first Stefan merely wondered why the surgeon was stalling. Then he grew depressed: the chances for a successful operation were decreasing every day.

The state of excitement passed. The engineer was able to sit in a chair. Pale and unshaven, he was the shadow of the burly man who had arrived three weeks earlier. His eyesight was gradually failing. Stefan no longer dared to ask about the date of the operation. Kauters was obviously upset, as if waiting for something to happen. Rabiewski had become his favorite patient, and the surgeon brought him lumps of sugar and sat watching him smack his lips and try to orient himself in relation to his own body, touching his thigh, his calf, his foot. His senses were slowly declining, and the world was fading for him. If you screamed into his ear, his twitching eyelids indicated that he could still hear.

On June 10, Kauters stuck his head out the door and called

87

Stefan in from the corridor. The room was almost empty: no table or chairs. Rabiewski was back in his net, swollen, naked, and huge.

"Pay close attention," Kauters said, beaming.

Rabiewski's body shuddered, his hands burrowing in the netting like unconscious animals. Then violent convulsions began. The cage screeched, its iron legs banging against the floor. The bed almost tipped over, and both doctors had to press it hard against the wall. The attack subsided as quickly as it had come. The body hung in the net like a board. Feverish shudders ran through an arm or a leg. Then this, too, ceased.

"Do you know what this is?" the surgeon asked Stefan, as if he were giving an examination.

"Irritation of the motor region caused by pressure from the tumor?"

Kauters shook his head. "No, my friend. The cortex has entered necrosis. An 'acortical man' is emerging. Freed from the cortex's inhibiting influence, the older, earlier evolved parts of the brain, still unaffected, are speaking up. That attack was Bewegungssturm, the motor storm, which occurs in all animals from infusorians to the birds. The animal is trying to escape, in the face of a threat to its life. The subsequent torpidity is the second stage of the same reactive apparatus. The so-called Totstellreflex, playing dead. Dung beetles do the same thing. See what it looks like? Now it's receding beautifully!" he cried, excited. The engineer, racked by cramps, was now arching his back, pressing against the nets.

"Yes . . . that comes from the quad protuberance. A classic case! The mechanism that served the amphibians millions of years ago now emerges in Homo sapiens when the more recently evolved parts of the brain drop away."

"Should I make the preparations for an operation?" Stefan

88

asked, unable to look either at the convulsing body or at the surgeon's joy.

"What? No, no. I'll let you know."

After his rounds, Stefan looked in on Sekułowski. Their relations had developed from their earlier unsettled state into a clearly established order: the master and the pupil who had to put up with his abuse. As a rule Stefan did not discuss patients with him, but Rabiewski was an exception: Stefan was desperate and needed advice. He dared not act on his own, and he was not sure what he could do anyway. Go to Pajączkowski? But that would mean lodging a complaint against Kauters, who was his superior and an experienced physician. So he settled on describing the engineer's condition to the poet, even if that might cause an outburst of passion and indignation. But Sekułowski himself had not been feeling well of late, and he was eager to hear the tale of someone worse off than he.

Plumping up the pillow behind his back, Sekułowski delivered a long exposition: "Once—maybe it was in 'The Tower of Babel,' I said that man presents a particular image to me. It is as if someone had labored for centuries to make the most beautiful golden sculpture, adorning every centimeter of its surface with varied forms: hushed melodies, miniature frescos, all the beauty of the world captured in a single totality obeying a thousand magical laws. And this sublime sculpture is mounted in the depths of a huge roiling dung heap. That, more or less, is man's position in the world. What genius, what precise craftsmanship! The beauty of the organs! The stubborn mind that harnesses the impassioned atoms, electron clouds, and wild elements, imprisons them in the body, and compels them to deeds alien to their nature. The infinite patience of designing the joints, the complex architecture of the bones, the labyrinth of circulating blood, the miraculous optical system, the finery of the fabric of nerves, thousands upon thousands of mutually restraining mechanisms, rising above anything we can think of. And all of it completely unnecessary!"

Stefan, shocked, was unable to reply. The poet smacked his hand against a large open book that had been covered by sheets of paper now strewn across the bedding: it was an anatomical atlas Stefan had lent him.

"What a disparity of means and ends. Your engineer vegetated, oblivious to what was fettered inside him, until suddenly the cells slipped their chains and their powers—until then directed inward, doing the bidding of kidneys and intestines—were suddenly liberated! The explosion of a thousand pent-up potentials. The spirit bursts through its chrysalis and appears in sudden enlargement: a watch with its works in revolt."

"Are you thinking of the malignancy?"

"That's what you call it. But what a name for it! You see, doctor, your ideas are pickled in formalin. For God's sake, show a little imagination! Cancer? That is simply the side door, the Seitensprung, of the organism. My Blind Powers, securing the living tissue against accidents of a hundred thousand kinds, seem to have left one vent ajar. Everything was working perfectly, and suddenly—out of control! Have you ever seen a child playing with a watch, the way the child pulls off the hour hand, which makes the second hand spin and buzz like a horsefly? Instead of measuring the hours, the hands gobble up fictitious time! A tumor is a little sprout that grows from one mutinous cell. Slowly, you understand? Slowly it develops in the brain, draws nourishment from the blood, invades, eats through, and destroys those well-tended flower gardens planted in the human fodder . . ."

"You may be right," said Stefan, "but why doesn't Kauters operate?"

90

The poet, writing so feverishly that his pen point kept making holes in the paper, did not reply. There was a long silence. Outside the window, a bronze ray broke through the clouds and lit the treetops. The room drank in the light, which abruptly vanished. Stefan's heart was pounding. Suddenly he asked, entirely out of context: "Excuse me. Why did you write *Reflections on Statebuilding?*"

Sekułowski, who had been lying on his side, turned and looked Stefan in the eye. Stefan could see the blood rising in the poet's face, but he still was glad that he had asked the question.

"What do you care?" Sekułowski retorted in a deep voice that Stefan had not heard before. "Please stop boring me! I have to write!"

And he turned his back on Stefan.

Stefan decided to see Staszek. Perhaps he could help.

Staszek tied a ribbon around the thesis he was working on and put it away in a drawer. He complained to Stefan. The hospital did not keep him busy, he was bored with the patients. It was an enormous effort to put in his hours. He could not walk, sit, or lie down; Nosilewska's image stayed with him constantly.

"You've got to make up your mind," Stefan said, overcome by sudden compassion. "If you want, I'll invite her to my room tonight, you come along, and then I'll say I have to get things ready for an operation and I'll leave you alone with her."

But Nosilewska declined the invitation. She was busy copying out data from a large German anatomy textbook. The green ink staining her fingertips made her look girlish. She said she had to go see Rygier right away. Rygier had once taught anatomy in medical school, and he could help her with some of this pathology material.

Staszek, who had been waiting in Stefan's room for the results of the expedition, now found new reasons to suffer. He was convinced that Rygier had invited Nosilewska for extra-scientific purposes.

"Well, maybe," Stefan thought. "Do you love her?"

Staszek shrugged. He was sitting sideways in the chair, his legs hanging over the arm, kicking nervously.

"I won't answer stupid questions. I can't work or read, I can't sleep, I've lost control of my thoughts, I'm going to hell in a handbasket, and that's it.

Stefan nodded. "It could be love. Let me ask you a couple of crucial questions. First, would you use her toothbrush?"

"Come on!"

"Yes or no."

Staszek hesitated. "Well, maybe yes."

"Do you feel a ripping and bursting in your chest, a divine fire?"

"Sometimes."

"Well, well. And now you're in a state because she's going to Rygier's? *Amor fulminans progrediens in stadio valde periculoso*. The diagnosis is a snap. No time for preventive measures. You need treatment."

Staszek looked at him gloomily. "Don't be a fool."

Stefan smiled because it had just occurred to him that if he wanted Nosilewska himself, he would have no trouble at all. "Don't get angry. I'll invite her tomorrow—or better yet, after the operation, once I get that off my mind."

"What do you mean? What's the difference what's on your mind?"

"Oh, so you're jealous of me too!" Stefan laughed. "I'll get some bromural for you, okay?"

"Thanks, but I have my own."

Staszek took a book from the shelf: *Magic Mountain*. He leafed through it, put it down, and took *The Green Python* instead.

"It's a detective story. Terrible," Stefan warned.

"So much the better. Then it'll fit my mood."

He headed for the door. Stefan's sympathy suddenly vanished. "Listen," he asked, "would you rather if she betrayed you or if something bad happened to her?"

"First, she can't betray me, because there's no connection between us. And anyway, what kind of choice is that?"

"It's a psychological test. Answer."

Staszek pushed the door open and slammed it as he rushed out. Stefan lay down on the bedspread in his clothes. Belatedly he realized that he had been angry with Staszek all evening because he had been unable to talk to him about the engineer. He got up, went to the shelf, and looked for the neurosurgery text. Maybe Kauters was doing the right thing. But he couldn't believe that. The text settled nothing. The sheer curtain rustled at the open window. Someone knocked at the door.

It was Kauters.

"Dr. Trzyniecki, please come to the operating room right away."

Stefan jumped up, but the surgeon was already gone, the fluttering folds of his unbuttoned smock disappearing into the dark corridor. Stefan ran down the stairs, forgetting to turn off the light in his room.

It was a warm, damp night. The wind carried the strong tickling smell of ripe grain. Stefan cut across the grass and ran up the iron steps to the second floor of the surgical wing, dew glistening on his shoes. White figures moved back and forth behind the frosted glass.

The operating room had begun as a small facility for procedures such as draining abcesses, to avoid having to transport patients to town. But there had been room for expansion, and Kauters had seized the opportunity. Now there was a table that could handle any kind of operation, along with oxygen

93

bottles, a wall-mounted electric bone cutter, and a diathermal unit that resembled an oversized radio. A short passageway, lined with the usual little yellow tiles, led to a second room where rows of chemical bottles, piles of rubber hoses, and linen under a glass bell stood on metal tables. Two wide cabinets held instruments neatly laid out on perforated trays. This corner full of sharp scalpels, hooks, and pincers glimmered even in the dark. Balls of catgut were soaking in amber lugol on a separate table. Rows of glass tubes containing white silk sutures shined on a shelf above.

Sister Gonzaga rolled the instrument cart up to the massive, three-legged operating table. Next she brought up the big nickel sterilizers, that looked like beehives on their high stands. Stefan was disoriented. He could not ask the nurse who the patient was. Gonzaga had already begun scrubbing up, so he threw on a long rubber apron and began to soap his hands under a roaring stream of water. Drops splashed onto the mirror and left opal tracks as they rolled down the mercury surface. White suds formed a ring in the basin.

Suddenly he heard Kauters's voice inside. "Take it easy, will you?" Then there was a deep sigh, as if someone was lifting a weight. Through the swinging doors, Stefan saw the bald head of the older male orderly, Joseph, who had Rabiewski's inert form draped over his shoulder. He set him down on the table with a bang.

Kauters, pulling on white rubber galoshes, asked the nurse, "Are the first and second sets ready?"

"Yes, doctor."

Tying the ribbons of his apron behind his neck, the surgeon stepped on the water pedal and began scrubbing up, his movements automatic.

"Are the syringes ready?"

"Yes, doctor."

94

"Make sure the needles are sharp."

He spoke mechanically, without even looking at the table. Joseph undressed Rabiewski, turned him onto his back, tied his arms and legs to handles with white straps, and began to shave his head with a straight razor, without lather. Stefan could not bear the dull scraping sound.

"For the love of God, Joseph, use a little soap and water!"

Joseph mumbled—when Kauters was around, he listened to no one else—but finally decided to moisten the engineer's head. Rabiewski's breathing was slow and shallow. Holding a few wisps of gray hair, Joseph attached a large anode pad to the patient's thigh and drew back from the table. Sister Gonzaga finished scrubbing with her third brush, dropped it into the bag, and walked toward the sterilizer with upraised hands. Joseph helped her on with a yellow mask, a coat, and thin fabric gloves. Next she went to the instrument stand, where three trays were still wrapped in the compresses in which they had come out of the autoclave. She unpinned the fabric and laid out the shining steel tweezers and rods in order of their importance.

Stefan and Kauters finished scrubbing at the same time. Stefan had to wait while the surgeon rinsed his hands in undiluted alcohol, and when his turn came, he held his fingers under the thin, stinging stream. Shaking his hands dry, he looked at them with concern.

"I have a splinter," he said, angrily touching the red spot near his fingernail. Kauters was putting on his rubber gloves, having a hard time with it because they were out of talc and his hands were wet.

"Don't worry. He certainly does not have PP. Anyway, things like that don't happen in the brain."

Joseph, unsterilized, was standing back from the table.

"Lights!" the surgeon commanded. Joseph threw a switch,

95

the transformer roared, and the large flat Jupiter angled over the table ringed them in a bluish light.

Kauters turned to the window for a moment. His face, masked up to the eyes, seemed darker than usual. The doctors approached the patient from opposite sides of the table. Joseph leaned nonchalantly against the sink, the reflection of his bald head like a sunflower in the mirror.

They began covering Rabiewski with compresses. Fishing them from the sterilizer with long forceps, Gonzaga was virtually hurling them into the surgeon's hands. The large squares of overlapping sterile cloth were laid from the patient's torso to his face. Stefan was pinning them together on the other side of the table.

"What are you doing? To the skin, to the skin!" the surgeon snapped sharply but quietly, plucking the fold of skin with his pincers. Though he had long grown accustomed to the sight of bodies being cut open, Stefan could never stop himself from shuddering when the compresses at the site of an operation were pinned to a patient's skin, even when he knew the patient was under anesthesia. And the engineer was merely unconscious. At just that moment the figure under the cloth trembled, grinding his teeth like flint scraping glass. Stefan automatically looked at Kauters. The surgeon looked back, then gestured as if to say: Go ahead and use a local anesthetic if it makes you happy.

After putting iodine on the portion of the head that stuck out of the tight ring of compresses, Stefan injected novocaine in several places and lightly rubbed the bumps the needle left on the skin. When Stefan had thrown away the iodine-stained pad, the surgeon reached back without looking. Sister Gonzaga placed the first scalpel in his hand. He touched the steel blade to the forehead, then made an oval incision. Kauters cleared away the connecting tissue down to the bone, using anatomical

96

pincers that made a dull grating sound. Then he laid the instruments on the patient's chest and reached for the trepan, an egg-shaped motor connected to an auger by a steel snake. Gonzaga stood immobile, several instruments in each raised hand. Stefan had just managed to blot the bright red streaks of blood around the incision when Kauters turned on the trepan. He held it like a pen. The auger bit into the bone, pitching out little particles that formed a line of bloody paste along the incision.

The buzzing stopped. The surgeon swung the auger away and called for a rasp. The plate of bone would not come free: it was sticking somewhere. Kauters pressed it delicately with three fingers, as if trying to push it into the skull.

"Chisel!"

He set the chisel at an angle and tapped it with a wooden hammer. Streams of blood wound along the skin and the compresses slowly turned crimson. Suddenly the plate of bone trembled. Kauters worked the rasp under it and leaned. There was a sharp crack like a nutshell breaking. The plate flipped over and fell off.

The meninges, the membrane surrounding the brain, swelled and glinted in the light. A network of dark veins could be seen in its depths. Kauters moved his hand away and came back with a long needle. He pricked the membrane in several places, once, twice, three times.

"Just as I thought," he murmured. Above his mask, his glasses reflected a miniature image of the lamp. Until that moment, Stefan had been applying sterile pads to stanch the flow of blood into the wound. Now he leaned forward. Their gauze-capped heads touched.

Kauters hesitated. Holding his left hand at the edge of the incision, he touched the membrane delicately with his right. The brain underneath, pulsing gray and pink, showed more clearly. Kauters looked up as if he expected a sign from above. His large black eyes looked so vacant that Stefan was almost frightened. Kauters ran his rubber-covered finger twice around the exposed membrane in a circle.

"Scalpel!"

It was a small, special knife. At first the membrane would not yield, but suddenly it split like a blister and brain burst through from below. It throbbed, swelling red in the tear from which viscid threads of blood trickled.

"Knife!"

Now there was a new sound, a bass rumbling of the dia-thermal apparatus. Gonzaga unwound the gauze from the elec-tric knife and placed it in Kauters's hand. Both doctors leaned forward. The flow of blood was not significant; no major vessels had been severed. But the situation was murky. Slowly, mil-limeter by millimeter, Kauters widened the opening in the membrane. At last, everything was clear: the protruding, swol-len part was the forward pole of the frontal lobe. When the surgeon poked at it with his finger, the yellow tumor appeared deep in the cleft between the two hemispheres. Getting to it would be difficult. He slid his index finger along the bulging folds of the cortex. He finally managed to reach the growth with the pincers. The tumor lay at the base of the skull, which for an instant showed pearly-blue like the inside of a seashell; then blood covered it. The tumor extended in both directions, compact at the bottom and plump at the top. It was covered with a brown paste.

"Scoop!"

Kauters began raking out blood-soaked scraps, threads, and strips. Then suddenly he jerked back. Stefan froze for an in-stant before he understood what had happened. A needle-thin stream of blood was shooting straight up from the bottom of the wound, from between the two hemispheres of the brain that the surgeon was holding apart with his fingers. An artery. Kauters blinked. Several drops had hit him in the eye.

"Damn it!" he said. "Gauze!"

Blood saturated the tampon, part of the tumor remained, and it was impossible to see anything. Kauters pulled his belly back from the table, looked up at the ceiling, and moved his finger around in the wound. This continued as the compresses soaked up blood, which seeped onto the pads put down at the beginning of the operation. New compresses were added because hands and instruments were getting slippery. Stefan stood looking at Kauters, helpless. His mask had slipped and was pressing against his nose, but he could not touch it.

The surgeon turned on the diathermal apparatus with the foot pedal and moved the knife closer.

Blood throbbed visibly in the mangled tissue of the tumor. Then the first faint blue smoke of scorched protein rose and Stefan smelled the characteristic stench through his gauze mask. The hemorrhage stopped. Only where tweezers had been left clamped in the wound did tiny red drops crawl like ants.

"Scoop!"

The operation continued. The surgeon ran the thermocoagulator over the tumor's surface. When it had cooled and solidified, he spooned it out, going after the remains with a crooked finger. But the longer this went on, the worse things got. The tumor pushed the lobe upward and pressed into it. The surgeon worked more and more briskly. At one point, reaching deep into the wound, he shuddered: when he pulled his hand out, the glove was ripped. The yellow rubber peeled back from his finger, cut by a sharp edge of bone.

"Shit!" Kauters said in a dull voice. "Please get this off for me."

"A new pair, doctor?" asked Gonzaga, instantly lifting a packet from the sterilizer with a fluid movement of her forceps.

"The hell with it!"

Kauters ground the strips of rubber into the floor. His anger gathered in the wrinkles around his eyes, and shiny bluish drops of sweat sparkled on his narrow brow. The muscles at his temples bulged: he was grinding his teeth. He moved his fingers more and more brutally in the wound, pulling out and tossing aside ragged scraps, necrotic tissue, and the burst remains of some vessel. The floor was spattered with bloody commas and question marks.

The clock read ten: the operation had lasted an hour so far.

"Take a look at his pupils."

Stefan lifted the sheet, which was heavy and stiff with coagulation, soaked with red blotches. Rabiewski's face was shiny, pale as paper, as Stefan lifted his eyelids with tweezers. The pupils were tiny. Suddenly the patient's eyes danced wildly, as if someone was pulling them on a string.

"Well?" Kauters asked.

"Nystagmus," said Stefan, stupefied.

"Yes, of course."

Kauters's voice sounded derisive. He was drawing a needle across the cortex. The brain was deeply open, and there was more and more necrotic mass, fusing with the spirals and convolutions. Stefan looked at the wound, which gaped like an open mouth. He could see the white tissue of nerves shining like a hulled walnut and the gray matter, which was actually brownish, with lighter, narrow smears. Drops of blood shined like rubies here and there.

Irritated, the surgeon drew a convolution sideways; it stretched like rubber. "Let's finish up!" he barked.

That meant he was giving up. His fingers worked quickly now, deftly pushing as much as possible of the bulging hemisphere back into the cavity of the skull. Bleeding started again somewhere. Kauters touched the dark end of the electric knife

100

to a vessel and stanched the hemorrhage. But suddenly he froze.

Stefan, who had been staring at the mummy-like figure on the table during this last procedure, understood. Rabiewski's chest had stopped moving. Without worrying about infecting his hand, the surgeon grabbed the bottom of the sheet covering the patient's chest and face, tugged it aside, listened for a moment, and walked silently from the table. He kicked his bloody rubber galoshes off against the wall. Gonzaga took the edge of the sheet and drew it sacramentally over the stricken face. Stefan went to the window to catch his breath. Gonzaga was collecting the instruments on metal trays behind him, water roared in the autoclave, and Joseph mopped blood from the floor. Stefan stood leaning on the window ledge. A great, silent darkness spread before him. At the junction of sky and earth, he thought, loomed something darker than the night. The warehouses of Bierzyniec shined like a diamond necklace against dark fur. The wind faded in the trees and the stars trembled. The last of the water gurgled in the drain.

Woch the
Substation Operator

June was edging toward a heat wave. The forests, malachite
green and fawn, shaded the view of the hills. There were silver
birches, sodden evenings, and crystal dawns. Birds chirped
endlessly. One evening the first thunderstorm struck. The
landscape gleamed in the flashes of lightning.

Stefan went for long walks in the fields near the woods. The
telegraph poles hummed like drunken tuning forks.

When he tired, he would rest under a tree or sit on a bed
of pine needles. One day, as he wandered, he found a place
where three great beech trees grew above a bare patch of
ground. They rose from a single stump and leaned gently away
from one another. Nearby was an oak tree, not as tall, its
branches forming horizontal, Japanese lines. It seemed to be
standing on tiptoe, for the spring rains had washed the earth
from between its roots. The forest ended a few hundred feet
farther on. A row of beehives painted green and red like roadside shrines seemed to march up the hill. There was an echo;
Stefan clapped his hands and the hot air answered several
times. The buzzing of the bees underlined the silence. Now
and then, a hive would sing more insistently. He walked on

and was surprised to find that the buzzing of the beehives, far from fading, was growing louder. A deep humming filled the air.

When the gorge he was walking through rose to the level of the surrounding meadow, Stefan found himself near a square brick building that looked like a box on short concrete legs. Rows of wooden poles strung with wires led away from the building in three directions; the sound was coming from an open window. As he came closer, Stefan saw two men sitting on the grass in the shade below the window. He gave a start because at first he thought that one of them was his cousin Grzegorz, whom he had not seen since the funeral in Nieczawy. But then he realized that it was the stranger's fair hair, the way he held his head, and his soldier's uniform with the insignia ripped off that accounted for the resemblance. Stefan left the path and walked across the grass, gazing into the distance so as to look like an aimless wanderer. The others did not notice him until he was quite close. Then they looked up and Stefan met two pairs of eyes. He stopped. There was an uncomfortable silence. The man he had taken for Grzegorz sat still, his arms resting on his knees and his muddy boots crossed; a bronze triangle of naked chest was visible under his unbuttoned shirt, and his coppery hair covered his head like a helmet. He squinted as he turned his thin, hard face toward Stefan. The other man was older. Big but not fat, he had ash-colored skin. He wore a cap with the visor turned to the back, and he was missing an ear. In its place was a tiny, twisted flap of red flesh, sticking out like a flower petal.

"Is this a power station?" Stefan finally asked to end the silence. The only sound was the humming from the window. Then he noticed that a third person, a pale old man, was standing inside the window. His dark blue work-suit made him almost invisible against the dim interior. The young man glanced up at him and then back at Stefan. Without looking him in the eye, he said ominously, "You better stay away from here."

"What?" Stefan said.

"I said you better stay away. Or there might be trouble."

But the man missing an ear cut him off. "Hold it. Where are you from, sir?"

"The hospital. I'm a doctor. Why?"

"Aaah," drawled the man without the ear, settling down with his elbow on the grass so he could talk more comfortably. "Do you take care of those—you know?" He pointed a finger to his temple and made a rotating gesture.

"Yes."

The man without the ear laughed. "Well, I guess it doesn't matter."

"I'm not allowed to walk here?" Stefan asked.

"Sure. Why not?"

"I mean," Stefan said, completely confused, "isn't this a power station?"

"No," said the old man in the window. Copper wires shined behind him. He leaned out the window to clean his pipe, and his forearms, covered with a tracing of veins, poked out beyond his short sleeves. "No, it's only a sixty-kilowatt substation," he said, concentrating on his pipe.

Stefan pretended that he knew what that meant and asked, "You supply current to the hospital, then?"

"Mmm," answered the old man, sucking in his cheeks as he tried his pipe.

"Look, can I walk around here or not?" Stefan asked, not knowing why he needed reassurance.

"Why not?"

"Because he said . . ." and Stefan turned to the young man, who broke into a wide smile that showed his sharp teeth.

"So I did," he said.

When Stefan did not leave, the man without the ear apparently decided to clear things up. "How was he supposed to know who you were, sir?" he said. "You made a mistake, kid. But if I may say so, sir, your face is pretty dark. That's why."

Seeing that Stefan still hadn't got the point, he touched him amiably on the knee. "He thought you were from Bierzyniec. That you were one of the ones being shipped out all over the place." He gestured as if he was draping something over his right shoulder and it finally dawned on Stefan: He thought I was a Jew. That had happened before.

The man without the ear was watching Stefan's reaction closely, but Stefan said nothing. He only blushed slightly. The other man made conversation to cover the awkward silence.

"You work in the hospital, doctor?" he asked. "Well I work here. My name's Woch. Operator. But not lately, because I've been sick. Too bad I didn't know about you, doctor," he added. "I would have asked for some advice."

"Were you sick?" Stefan asked pleasantly. He stood there, for some reason unable to walk away. It was his misfortune never to know how to strike up a conversation with a stranger or how to end one.

"I was sick. The way it happened, first one eye pointed this way and the other one that way, then everything started to go around and around, and my sense of smell got so—ah!"

"And then?" Stefan felt foolish listening to the description.

"Nothing. It just went away by itself."

"Not by itself," the old man in the window said.

"All right, not by itself," Woch loyally corrected himself. "I ate pea soup so thick you could stand the spoon in it, with sausage, marjoram, and a shot of whiskey, and it went away. My friend's advice—the guy there."

"Very good," said Stefan, nodding to each of them and walking quickly away, because he was afraid that Woch would ask him what the illness had been.

He looked back when he got to the top of the first hill. The little red house stood there at the bottom of the gorge, seemingly uninhabited. The low humming from the open window, fading steadily, stayed with him most of the way back to the asylum, until it could no longer be distinguished from the buzzing of the insects above the warm grass.

This incident stuck in Stefan's memory, as if it had some hidden meaning. So distinctly did he remember it that it divided the past into two parts and was his reference point for the chronology of hospital events. He told no one about it: that would have been pointless. Perhaps Sekułowski might have found some literary merit in Woch's description of his illness, but that hardly mattered to Stefan. What did matter? He could not say.

After his morning rounds he would go for walks, carrying *The History of Philosophy*. But since he was making slow progress (unwilling to admit that ontological subtleties bored him, he blamed the hot weather), he began carrying another book: a thick edition of the *Thousand and One Nights* in a beautiful pale binding. It was from Kauters's library. He would sit in that picturesque spot in the woods under the three tall beeches with their smooth, tight bark, imagining that a rubber tree must be similar. Feet propped on a log overgrown with blueberries, squinting at the flashes of sun that danced above the yellowed pages, he read the adventures of the peddlers, barbers, and wizards of Baghdad while *The History of Philosophy* lay beside him on a clump of dried moss. He no longer even bothered to open it, but carried it along like a guilty conscience.

One day when it was oppressively hot even deep in the forest, he was reading the story in which the caliph Harun al-Rashid disguised himself as a poor water-carrier to loiter in the marketplace and find out more about his subjects. Stefan suddenly thought how much fun it would be to go to the substation disguised as a worker. He rejected the idea with embarrassment, but regretted having no one to share it with.

In the evenings, when the sun went down and a breeze began to flutter between the hills, Stefan would leave the sanitorium again. With a spark of hidden excitement, he would turn off the path and circle the substation at a distance. But he never ran into anyone.

He never headed straight for the little brick house; it was enough to catch a remote glimpse of its red walls and the open window from which the steady hum came. These wanderings showed up in his dreams: several times he saw the house in the meadow; it called to him with a sound of oriental music. One morning he walked out earlier than usual to look at the substation from the ridge. Before he got there, he saw someone coming toward him along the path. It was the young, copper-haired worker, wearing lime-spotted trousers, stripped to the waist, carrying two buckets of earth but tramping energetically under the load. Stefan wasn't sure whether he wanted to meet him, but he slowed down. The other man's muscles rippled under his skin as he came down the path, but his face was indifferent, expressionless. So deliberately did he fail to look at Stefan as he passed that Stefan, certain that he had been recognized, dared not look back as the man continued in the other direction.

About a week later, Stefan was on his way back from the nearby town, where he had done some afternoon shopping. The heat was stifling. There had been rumbling from beyond the horizon for an hour, but the sky overhead was clear. The dirt road felt as hard as concrete after baking in the sun for

107

days. Stefan suddenly noticed a wall of clouds above a clump of firs. The landscape was darkening before his eyes, and he quickened his steps in the gloom, until he came panting around a bend and saw Woch the Operator up ahead of him. Woch was going in the same direction but more slowly, pushing a bicycle along by the handlebars. When he heard steps behind him, he turned, recognized Stefan, and said hello. They walked side by side in silence for some time.

Woch was wearing dirty boots, a sweater, and a jacket with the collar turned up. Though Stefan was sweating heavily in a shirt and linen trousers, the man showed no sign of discomfort. His face was as expressionless and gray as usual, except for the red flap where his ear had been. Yellow clouds roiled above them. Stefan would happily have broken into a run, but it somehow inhibited him that Woch was marching along at such an even pace.

The road widened and came up even with its banks. They had turned off onto a sandy path when the first big drops began pocking the dust at their feet. The substation was in sight.

"Why don't you come with me? It's going to pour," Woch said. Stefan agreed. They made for the substation without a word. Heavy drops hit Stefan's hands and face and blotted his shirt and trousers.

A few steps from the door, Woch stopped and looked back, leaning on the handlebars. Stefan also turned. A shelf of turbulent black-bottomed cloud was heading toward them, streams of it reaching down toward the ground.

"Where I come from, they call that a male cloud," Woch said, squinting at the sky. Stefan wanted to laugh, but Woch's face was gloomy. Then the downpour broke with a roar.

Stefan got inside the substation in two bounds. Woch, water streaming off him, seemed to defy the rain and deliberately lifted first the front, then the rear wheel of the bicycle into the

108

building. Only when it rested against the wall did he take out a handkerchief and carefully wipe his eyes and cheeks.

Through the open door they could see the gray deluge drowning everything in sight. Stefan inhaled the wonderfully cool air deeply, delighted to have escaped the flood. Only when Woch opened a second, inner, door did he realize that he had been granted a unique opportunity.

He followed Woch into the building's main, modestly sized room. Rain beat against the three windows, and it would have been dark but for the ceiling lamps. Their steady light revealed a stand against one wall and a control board with gauges; the opposite wall looked like a zoo. It consisted of cages made of wire screens painted gray; they stood side by side and extended to the ceiling. Stefan could not tell what was in the narrow cages, but it was certainly nothing alive, for there was no movement. In the middle of the room stood a small table, two chairs, and several boxes. A rubber mat covered the stone floor.

"Isn't there anyone here?" Stefan asked.

"Pościk's here. It's his shift. Please wait. And don't touch anything!"

Woch went to a door in the corner of the room where the screens ended, opened it, looked inside, and said something. Stefan heard a muffled reply. Woch went in and closed the door behind him. Stefan was alone for perhaps a minute. The dull indeterminate hum filled the air, which was thick with the smell of hot oil, and the rain whipped across the tin roof in waves.

As he looked around, Stefan noticed something shining behind the metal screens. He moved closer and in the darkness saw vertical copper rails and the knobs of porcelain insulators. Then he heard voices from behind the wall.

"Have you been drinking, Władek?" Woch was saying. "You want to take it out now?"

"Let's wait outside," said a second, lower voice.

"Outside. If it doesn't work, we're dead anyway. Do you realize how much there is? Get out, right now!"

"Okay, Jasiu, okay. Jasiu, in the woods maybe?"

"In the woods, wonderful! Come on, we have a guest."

"What?"

The voices dropped to an indistinct murmur. Stefan quickly moved back to the center of the room. Woch and old Pościk came in. They both looked at the gauges. The operator said something, but a crash of thunder drowned him out. Woch took a few steps, stopped on tiptoe, and looked again at the apparatus.

"Well?" asked the old man.

The answer was a wave of the hand that signaled: forget it. Woch bowed his head, held his own shoulders with his hands across his chest, and slowly rocked back on his heels, standing as Stefan imagined a ship's captain would when braving a storm. Then Woch noticed Stefan and gave a start. He picked up a chair, carried it through the door, and put it down in the corridor saying, "Please sit here. You'll be safe here."

Stefan obeyed. The door to the room was open, creating a strange sort of stage, Stefan sitting in the dark narrow corridor, the only spectator.

The two men inside weren't doing anything. The old man sat on a box, while Woch remained standing. No longer watching the apparatus, they seemed to be waiting for something. Their faces glowed more and more brightly in the yellow lamplight; Stefan felt nauseated from the oppressive smell of oil; outside, the storm roared and thundered with steady intensity. At one point Woch rushed to the black stand and looked closely at a gauge, then at another, before returning to his place and sinking back into immobility. Stefan began to feel disappointed—but then he sensed some changes, though he did not know how. His uneasy impression mounted until he suddenly discovered its source.

110

There was movement in the depths of the cages along the wall. He heard a kind of scraping, a hiss; it grew to an impatient gnashing, fell quiet, then came back. Woch and Pościk, must have heard it, for they both looked around, and the old man glanced at Woch with what Stefan thought was fear. Yet neither of them moved.

Minutes passed as the rain beat on the roof and the low electric hum persisted, but the noise coming from the cages did not let up. Something was rustling, scraping, buzzing, as if a living being was dashing about and pushing in all directions: the strange sounds came from opposite ends of the cage in turn, from the bottom and then from the top near the ceiling. The mysterious thing seemed to be jerking more and more violently behind the steel screen. A blue flash suddenly filled two of the cages, grew stronger, casting distorted shadows of the two men against the opposite wall, then vanished. An acrid, searing smell burned Stefan's nostrils. There was another sharp hiss and a crackling flame winked in the depths of another cage; a flurry of sparks shot from the metal bar that stuck out under the screen.

Old Pościk stood up, stuffed his pipe into his apron pocket, and, standing rigidly erect, looked silently at Woch. The operator grabbed him tightly by the arm and, his face twisted into what could have been anger, shouted something that was swallowed up by the clap of a nearby thunderbolt. A sudden flash ripped through three of the cages, extinguishing the lights for an instant, and the whole wall looked as if it was on fire. Woch pushed the old man toward Stefan and with his hands in front of him slowly went to the control panel. It sounded as though someone was shooting a pistol in the cages, and blue and red flames poured through the screens. Choking on the smell of ozone, Stefan backed off down the corridor, stopping at the door. The old man hunched beside him and Woch, after taking a last look at the apparatus, sprang after them

111

with a youthful stride. They stood together in the corridor. Things quieted down behind the screens. A few small blue flames still danced in the corners. The thunder was receding, but the rain still drummed steadily on the roof.

"It's over," the old man finally said, taking the pipe out of his pocket. His hands seemed to be trembling, but it was too dark to tell.

"Well, we're still alive," Woch said. He walked back into the room, stretched as though awakening from a good sleep, slapped his hands against his hips, and sat down abruptly on a stool.

"It's all right now," he nodded to Stefan, "you can come in."

The thunder stopped completely but the rain still fell as though it might go on forever. The old man shuffled around the room, making notes on a sheet of graph paper. Then, opening a door in the corner that Stefan had not noticed, he disappeared inside and rummaged around, making a lot of noise that sounded like metal clattering. He came back carrying a frying pan, a spirit stove, and a pot of peeled potatoes. He put things on the table and the floor and set about preparing a meal. Murmuring "What can I offer you" over and over, he tiptoed around, disappeared, came back, put the pan on, and, enveloped in a cloud of burning fat, broke and sniffed the eggs with an expression of devout concentration. In the meantime, Woch formally invited Stefan to wait out the rain in the substation.

Stefan asked what had happened. Woch explained about the lightning rods that protected them, about circuit breakers, and about the excess current, and although Stefan did not understand everything, he felt that something else had happened and that Woch was minimizing the danger for reasons known only to himself. Stefan had no doubt that there had

112

been danger—he could tell that from the way the two operators had acted. Woch showed him around the room, naming all the equipment, and even let him look into the back room where he had first gone to talk to Pościk. An iron drum hung on the wall with copper rails leading down from it, and on the floor was a large container full of coils which, Woch explained, would protect against fire if the drum, which was a breaker, sprayed out burning oil.

"What's under the coils?" asked Stefan, trying to sound reasonable and relevant.

Woch looked at him coolly. "Why should anything be under the coils? There's nothing."

They went back to the room. A small bottle of eighty-proof vodka and a sliced pickle had appeared on the table. Woch poured out tiny glasses, drank to Stefan's health, then corked the bottle and hid it behind a pillar, announcing: "Vodka is bad for us."

He said nothing more about what had happened during the storm, but he got friendlier. He ignored the old man, as if he were not even there. He took off his jacket and hung it over the back of his chair. His gray sweater stretched across his chest. He took out a tin tobacco box and some cigarette papers and offered them to Stefan. "It's strong," he warned.

Stefan tried to roll a cigarette, eventually producing a crooked weed whose ragged ends he licked so hard that the tobacco fell out. Woch, who had been pretending not to watch, took a paper and a pinch of sawdust-like tobacco between two stubby fingers, snapped his thumb up, and handed Stefan a cigarette ready to be licked. Stefan thanked him and bent over Woch's lighter. The flame nearly burned his eyebrows, but Woch deftly moved it aside. The first puff choked Stefan, tears came to his eyes, but he tried his best to look natural. Woch pretended not to notice again. He made another cigarette for

113

himself, lit it, and they sat silently as the smoke merged into a single blue cloud under the lamp above their heads.

"How long have you been working in this field?" Stefan asked, realizing that the question might sound foolish but unable to think of anything else. The operator puffed on his cigarette as if he had not heard, then suddenly slapped his hand down.

"I went to work when I was a boy this high," he said, holding out his hand. "No, this high," he said, lowering it. "In Malachowice. They didn't have electricity yet. The French came to set up the turbines. The foreman was an honest man. When he shouted in the boiler room, you could hear him out on the ramp. But he didn't scream at kids, he was patient and tried to teach them. The first time you went up on the high-tension circuit-breaker to dust it off—because that's how you start— he'd show you the brush with the dead man's hand on it. You never forgot that."

"I don't understand," Stefan said.

"Just a regular paintbrush. Horsehair. That's what you use to dust. But the current has to be off in the cables, no tension. If you forget and touch a live cable, flame shoots out and that's it. Anyway, this was a brush from someone who forgot. A guy fresh from the village. I didn't know him, he was before my time. His fingerprints were burned into the handle, black as coal. In fact, the corpse was black as coal from head to toe. Burned to a crisp.

"Anyway," Woch went on, "that's the way to do it. Nobody ever learned our trade from talking. Good eyes, good hands— that's what you need. And always look alive. I liked the work. And my boss liked me. I went from low voltage to high voltage. I worked on the lines for a while, but my heart wasn't in it. The lines aren't for me. Put on the irons, climb up, climb down, pull the lines, over and over again, from pole to pole.

Everyone gets sick of it, so they have to keep hiring new people. Vodka is the only joy in that work. One mistake, one wrong cable, and bang! Everlasting glory."

The half-finished cigarette stuck to his lip so he had both hands free, though he wasn't using them at the moment.

"I worked with a guy named Józef Fijałka. All he did was drink. He was already drunk by the time he got to work and he never talked, just mumbled, but he was a good worker as long as he was on his feet. He drank from payday until his money was gone. The first half of the month, he was an angel, the second half, the hell with him. Once he disappeared right after payday. They looked everywhere and finally found him in the switching station. He'd gone to sleep right between the high-tension cables, but he was drunk and nothing happened. They picked him up by the legs and pulled him out. Very carefully. Eventually he got himself killed. It was on a transformer. I went to see him in the hospital, and he was covered with bandages. He asked me to lift up his arm, and when I did, there was nothing in his armpit. Just bones. All the flesh was gone. He died fast."

Woch paused and took a drag of his cigarette. He fell into a reverie.

"The union paid for the funeral, and they did right by his family too. That's how it used to be. Later on, in the thirties, they started laying men off."

He crushed out his cigarette with a look of disgust.

"I had a repair crew working under me. You sit around all night waiting. A bird lands on a line and gets fried, a branch falls and knocks something down, a kid shorts something out flying a kite. All that stuff is natural. But then in the thirties this new thing started. I'll never forget the first one. Not as long as I live. Suicide. A kid tied a wire around a stone, held the other end of the wire in his hand, and threw the stone over the cables. He was burned completely black, his hand fell off, and the fat that melted off him was strewn all around. If I hadn't known him—but I did. He worked in the railroad yards, but they laid him off because he wasn't married. They laid the bachelors off first. The girls liked him, he was a nice kid. People hadn't known that electrocution was a quick death, but now they found out. And it was easy too, especially since the French ran the cables next to footbridges. It was cheaper that way. Very economical, the French. All you needed was a stone, a wire, and an easy toss."

Woch was holding onto the edge of the table, as if he wanted to lift it.

"After that, every time the telephone rang when I was on duty, my heart stopped. By the time the third goddamned one did it, the whole city knew. There was an employment office right near the power station. We'd go out there, and they were lined up like sheep—the unemployed. Somebody once shouted, 'There go the pallbearers!' Pieluch, my assistant, shouted back, 'Jump in the goddamn river, and we won't have to bother.' When they heard that, that was it. It's a good thing we had a good driver, because the stones were flying. That Pieluch and I had words after that. He was no operator, but he had a sick wife. I could have had a hundred better men instead of him, and that made me angry. 'You were rotting away down there a week ago yourself,' I told him, 'and now that you've had a couple of days' work you say the hell with the rest of them.' He was hot-tempered. He came back at me. So I busted him in the mouth. Later he came in begging for his job because his wife was dying and he didn't have any money, but what could I do? And his wife really did die on him. That fall. When he came back from the funeral, he stuck his head through the window—I was on duty—and said, very quietly, 'Die a slow death!' Less than a week later, we got

116

another call to go out to the bridge for a suicide, and damned if it wasn't him. Baked like a goose. You could've stuck your finger in his chest. It was roasted crisp."

The old man put two tin bowls of thick soup on the table and sat on a box nearby, balancing a steaming pot on his knees. They ate slowly. Stefan burned his tongue on the first spoonful. He blew on the next one. When they finished, Woch brought the tin box of tobacco out again. They smoked. Stefan was hoping that the operator would keep on telling stories, but he didn't seem to feel like it. He sat there gray, massive, and gloomy, breathing heavily, exhaling smoke, parrying Stefan's questions with monosyllables. When Stefen found that Woch had worked at the power station in his home town for a few years, he remarked, "So it was thanks to you that I had lights at home." He wanted to emphasize this as a bond that would always connect them.

Woch said nothing, as if he had not heard. The rain had almost stopped, just a few drops falling from the eaves outside the window. Stefan hesitated to leave; he did not want to part from Woch in the mood of distance that had arisen. The conversation had petered out, and Stefan, looking for a new theme, picked up Woch's engraved nickel lighter from the table. "Andenken aus Dresden" was engraved on one side in Gothic script. He turned it over and read, "Für gute Arbeit."

"A beautiful lighter," he said. "Did you work in Germany too?"

"No," said Woch, staring straight ahead, his eyes blank. "The boss gave it to me."

"German?" Stefan asked, a bit unpleasantly.

"German," Woch confirmed, looking closely at Stefan.

"For good work," Stefan said with a barely perceptible sneer, though he was well aware that this was not going to improve the mood.

117

"That's right, for good work," Woch replied emphatically, almost belligerently. Stefan had lost any sense of how to approach Woch. He stood up and, feigning nonchalance, strolled around the room, walking close to the equipment, willing to expose himself to a harsh rebuke about safety, anything to break the hostile silence. But in vain. The old man noisily gathered up the dirty dishes, carried them away, came back, and started speaking to Woch in indistinct syllables that Stefan could not follow. Woch sat there, bent forward, leaning his heavy chest against the edge of the table. The electricity hummed and the fresh cool of evening blew in through the open window. The young worker Stefan had seen twice before came in from the corridor. The army coat, turned inside out, covered his back; his copper hair stuck to his skull and streams of water ran down his face. A little puddle formed at his feet where he stood in the doorway. Though no one spoke, it was clear they were expecting him. They exchanged meaningful glances, the old man shuffled off to the corner, and Woch stood up briskly and walked over to Stefan. "I'll show you out, doctor," he said. "You can go now."

It was so blunt, so completely devoid of politeness, that all Stefan's efforts to appear to leave of his own volition collapsed. Hurt, angry, he let himself be led outside. Woch pointed toward the hospital. Stefan blurted, "Mr. Woch, you know why I came, I . . ."

It was so dark that they could not see each other's faces. "Don't worry," Woch said quietly, "I couldn't let you get soaked. It was only natural. Otherwise, there's really nothing much to see here. Unless . . . You understand." He put his hand lightly on Stefan's shoulder, not as a gesture of confidence, but simply to make sure where he was in the darkness between them.

Stefan, who did not understand, said, "Yes, yes. Well,

thanks, and good night." He felt a brief squeeze of the other man's hand, turned; and walked straight ahead.

He trudged up the dirt path. Gusts of wind bore scattered raindrops. He felt flushed after his adventure—a few hours that loomed larger than his months at the hospital. His anger at Woch had dissolved when they parted in the darkness, and now he only regretted that he had been so stupid, but what else could he have done but ask naive questions? He felt like a child trying to decipher the mysterious actions of adults. Just when he thought he had been initiated into the first mystery, they had thrown him out. For a moment he longed to go back and watch the three of them through the window. Of course he would not have dared, but the thought testified to his state of mind. He told himself that nothing unusual would be going on at the substation, that the others would be asleep and Woch would be sitting in the bright light among the equipment, getting up to look at the gauges now and then, entering some note on graph paper, and sitting down again. It was futile and uninteresting. But why did his thoughts keep returning to that silent, monotonous work? He suddenly found himself at the dark main gate, fumbling with his key in the wet lock. Blindly he followed the path that was a shade lighter than the surrounding dark grass and made his way to his room. He undressed without turning on the light and jumped under the covers. When he touched the cold sheets, he felt that it would not be easy to fall asleep. He was right.

Of all the people who used to come to his father's workshop when he was a child, it was the workers who interested him most—the machinists, locksmiths, and electricians who made various parts to order. He had been intimidated by them—they were so different from everyone he knew. They were always patient, listening to his father with silent attention, looking at the blueprints carefully, almost respectfully. But beneath the cautious politeness lay something closed and hard. Stefan noticed that although his father liked to go on at the dinner table about people he had met, he never mentioned the workers, as if they, in contrast to the lawyers, engineers, and merchants, had no personality. Stefan had the illusion then that their life—"real life," as he called it—was shrouded in mystery. For some time he racked his brains over the puzzle of that "real life," before finally concluding that the idea was foolish.

Now, lying awake in the darkness, the memory surfaced. There had been some sense in that boyish dreaming after all: there was a real life for people like Woch!

Where Uncle Ksawery propounded atheism, Anzelm held grudges, his father invented, and Stefan read philosophy and talked to Sekułowski, reading and talking for months on end to recognize "real life"—that life was out there maintaining their world, shouldering it like Atlas, as inconspicuous as the ground beneath their feet. But no, he was mythologizing, because something like a mutual exchange of services went on: Anzelm knew about architecture, Sekułowski wrote, he and Ksawery treated the sick. Stefan suddenly realized that nothing would really change if all of them disappeared. Whereas without Woch and others like him, the world could not go on.

He rolled over, and some obscure impulse made him turn on the nightstand lamp. It was nothing, of course, but the light struck him as a symbol, a sign that Woch was on the job. The yellow light filling the impersonal room was somehow soothing; it ensured freedom for all tasks and thought. As long as it shined, it was possible to fantasize about worlds beyond the existing one.

I ought to get some sleep, he thought. This is going nowhere. As he reached for the switch again, he noticed an open book on the table—*Lord Jim*, which he had been reading. He flicked the switch and darkness surrounded him again. In a quick leap of association, he wondered whether Woch would ever read that book, but the idea was so ludicrous that he smiled in the gloom. Woch would never pick up such a book; he had no need to sail the oceans with Lord Jim. He would look on Conrad with contempt for solving on paper problems that he himself solved in reality. Who could say what it cost him, how much suffering and care went into his vigil over electric current? The "real life" of guarding the lamplight did not seem to bother him. And it was better for Stefan not to reach out to him or to think about him too much, because it only made it hard to fall asleep.

Stefan's thoughts drifted. In his mind he saw the little house struck by bolts of lightning in a raging storm. He saw Woch's sad gray face, his thick fingers instantly quelling an overload, and then he saw nothing at all.

Marglewski's
Demonstration

In the hot days of July, the hospital finally caught up with the influx of wartime casualties. A balance between admissions and discharges was reached. At noon, the overhead sun truncating the stubby shadows of the trees in the yard, patients wandered in their underwear. A primitive shower was arranged for them in the evenings with a pump worked by Joseph, the big peasant nurse with an old face and a young body.

Stefan was sitting in the ambulatorium, where sparks of sunshine glimmered like filaments in a quartz lamp. He was writing up the admission of an ex-prisoner from a concentration camp. Some stroke of luck had opened doors for this man that usually swung in only one direction.

Marglewski came down the corridor and looked in. He seemed interested in the case. He whistled. "A beautiful cachexia," and laid his hand on the head of the ragged little man, who looked like a pile of old linen in the room's shining whiteness. The man sat immobile on a swivel stool. Two lopsided furrows cut across his cheeks from his eyes and disappeared into his beard.

"Debility? An idiot?" asked Marglewski, keeping his hand

on the poor man's head. Stefan stopped writing and looked up in surprise.

Bright tears rolled down the patient's cold, purplish cheeks and into his beard.

"That's right," Stefan said, "an idiot."

He stood up, pushed the papers into a corner of the desk, and went to see Sekułowski. He began awkwardly, saying that he had changed his mind on certain points and that it was high time to shed some of his intellectual baggage.

"Some concepts are obsolescent," he said, trying to sweeten an avowal of cynicism. "I have just experienced a small catharsis."

"Last year" Sekułowski said, "Woydziewicz gave me some cherry vodka that produced a genuine catharsis on a large scale. I suspect him of having thrown in some cocaine." But when he saw Stefan's expression, he said, "But go on, doctor. I'm listening. You are seeking and you have hit the target. Insane asylums have always distilled the spirit of the age. Deviation, abnormality, and weirdness are so widespread in normal society that it is hard to get a handle on them. Only here, concentrated as they are, do they reveal the true face of the times."

"No, that's not what I'm talking about," said Stefan, suddenly feeling terribly lonely. He searched for words but could not find them. "No, in fact it's nothing," he said, backing up and leaving in a hurry, as if he feared the poet would detain him.

But Sekułowski was absorbed by a spider climbing the wall behind his bed. He swatted it with a book, and when it fell to the floor, he sat staring at the blot of fluttering, threadlike legs.

Returning along the corridor, Stefan ran into Marglewski, who invited him to his apartment. "I have a bottle of Extra

123

Dry," he said. "Why don't you drop in, and we can get rinsed out."

Stefan declined, but Marglewski took the rejection for mere politeness. "No, come on, don't be silly."

Marglewski's apartment was at the opposite end of the same corridor as Stefan's. It had gleaming furniture: a glass-topped desk one side of which leaned on prism-shaped drawers, the other on bent steel tubing that matched the frames of the chairs. It reminded Stefan of a dentist's waiting room. The pictures on the walls were framed in metal tubes. Pedantically arranged books, each with a white number on its spine, filled two walls. As Marglewski set the low table, Stefan mechanically pulled a book from the shelves and leafed through it. It was Pascal's *Provinciales*. Only the first two pages had been cut. His host opened a drawer in a contemporary sideboard to reveal sandwiches on white plates. After his third drink Marglewski got talkative. Vodka exaggerated his already vigorous gestures. He wrung his hands like a washerwoman when he said he had stained his coat and would have to have it cleaned. He pointed out boxes labeled with index cards along the windowsill. Sheets of cardboard were held together with colored clips. Marglewski, it turned out, was engaged in scientific research. With a show of reluctance, he opened a folder bursting with papers analyzing the effect of Napoleon's kidney stones on the outcome of the battle of Waterloo and the influence of hormones on the visions of the saints—here he drew a circle, meant to represent a halo, in the air above his head and laughed. He was sorry that Stefan was not a believer; what he needed was pure, naive people steeped in dogma.

"You spend all that time talking to Sekułowski?" he exclaimed. "Ask him why literature has its head in the clouds. Believe me, more than one great love has gone down the drain because the guy had to take a leak and, afraid to mention it

124

to his dearly beloved, expressed a sudden longing for solitude and sprinted off into the bushes. I've seen it happen."

Out of boredom more than interest, Stefan reached into the files. There were heaps of typescript in stiff covers. Marglewski kept talking, but disconnectedly, as if his mind was somewhere else. Sitting there hunched over, his nostrils flared as though he were sniffing for something, Marglewski looked like an old maid eager to confess the story of her one indiscretion.

He launched into a discourse so pompously laden with Latin that Stefan understood nothing. Marglewski's thin, nervous hands stroked the cover of one of the boxes impatiently before finally opening it. Curious, Stefan glanced inside. He saw a long list like a table of contents, and skimmed down it: "Balzac—hypomanic psychopath, Baudelaire—hysteric, Chopin—neurasthenic, Dante—schizoid, Goethe—alcoholic, Hölderlin—schizophrenic . . . "

Marglewski unveiled his secret. He had embarked on a great investigation of geniuses, and had even intended to publish portions of it, but unfortunately the war intervened.

He began to lay out large sheets with drawings depicting genealogies. He got more excited as he spoke, and his cheeks grew flushed. As he passionately enumerated the perversions, suicide attempts, hoaxes, and psychoanalytic complexes of great men, it occurred to Stefan that Marglewski himself might well be suffering from an abnormality that afforded him a dubious kinship with his subjects, a kind of ticket to the family of geniuses. He had scrupulously collected descriptions of their every lapse, researching and cataloguing their failures, tragedies, misfortunes, and catastrophes. He swelled with joy at the discovery of the slightest hint of impropriety among anyone's posthumous papers.

At one point, as Marglewski rummaged in a lower drawer for his latest treasure, Stefan interrupted him. "It seems to me," he said, "that great works arise not out of madness, but in spite of it."

He took one look at Marglewski and immediately regretted having spoken. The man looked up over the papers and glared at him. "In spite of?" he sneered. Suddenly he gathered up the scattered papers, jerked a tattered chart away from Stefan, and nervously stuffed it back into a folder.

"My dear colleague," he said, interlacing his fingers, "you are still inexperienced. But this is no longer the age of the Renaissance man. For that matter, thoughtless actions could have fatal consequences even then. Of course you fail to understand this, but things that can be justified subjectively often look different in the light of the facts."

"What are you talking about?" Stefan asked.

Marglewski did not look at him. He wrung his long, thin fingers and stared at them. Finally, he said, "You take walks a lot. But those power-station operators in Bierzyniec with that building of theirs can only get the hospital into trouble. It's not only that they're hiding weapons, but that young one, Pościk's son, is nothing but a common bandit."

"How do you know?" Stefan interrupted.

"Don't ask."

"I don't believe it."

"You don't?" Marglewski peered through his glasses with an expression of pure hatred. "Haven't you heard of the Polish underground? The government-in-exile in London?" he asked in a shrill whisper, his long fingers running lightly over his white smock. "The army left weapons in the forest in September. That Pościk was in charge of them. And when he was ordered to tell where they were, he refused! Said he was waiting for the Bolsheviks!"

"He said that? How do you know?" Stefan asked, dazed by the unexpected turn of the conversation and by the way Marglewski was trembling.

126

"I don't know. I don't know anything! It's got nothing to do with me!" he said, still whispering. "Everyone knows about it—everyone except you!"

"I shouldn't go there anymore, is that what you mean?" Stefan stood up. "It's true I walked over there once, during a storm . . ."

"Say no more!" Marglewski cut him off, jumping to his feet. "Please forget this whole conversation! I thought it was my obligation to a colleague, that's all. Do what you think best with what I've told you, but please, don't say anything to anyone else!"

"Of course not," said Stefan slowly. "If that's what you want, I won't tell anyone."

"Let's shake on that!"

Stefan held out his hand. He was shocked by what Marglewski had said, and even more by his undisguised panic. Could someone have put the man up to it? What about his anger? Could he have something to do with the underground? Some sort of—what did they call it?—connection?

Stefan left in confusion. It was so hot that he had to keep wiping the sweat off his forehead as he walked down the corridor. He heard a loud burst of laughter from the toilet. The door opened and Sekułowski appeared, wearing only pajama bottoms, shaking with laughter that had seized him like the hiccups. Drops of sweat hung on the fair hairs of his chest.

"Perhaps you could share the joke?" asked Stefan, squinting against the light that poured through the corridor's glass roof and bounced off the walls, broken into rainbows.

Sekułowski leaned against the door, catching his breath.

"Doctor," he hawked finally, "doctor, it's just that . . ." He spoke in short bursts, gasping for breath. "It reminded me of our arguments, our learned . . . phenomena . . . the Upanishads, the stars, the soul, and when I saw that turd . . . I can't!" He

127

burst out laughing again. "Spirit? What is man? A turd! A turd!"

Gripped by his private delight, the poet walked away, still shaking with laughter. Stefan went to his room without a word.

His first inclination was to go to the substation and warn Woch. Stefan's promise meant nothing if honoring it would expose the operator to danger, but he knew immediately that he would not go. Who would he warn Woch about? Marglewski? Ridiculous. Tell him that weapons were hidden in the woods? If it was true, Woch would know more about it than he would.

He spent several days concocting increasingly elaborate ways of warning Woch to be careful: an anonymous note, another nocturnal meeting, but none of it made sense. In the end he did nothing. He did not go back to the substation, feeling an obligation to Woch not to, but he did begin to wander in its vicinity again. On his way out early one morning, he saw Joseph on one of the highest hilltops. The nurse was sitting motionless on the grass, as if absorbed by the picturesque view, but nothing Stefan knew about him indicated any weakness for the beauties of nature. Stefan watched him covertly for a while and then, seeing nothing interesting, turned back. He was already close to the hospital when it occurred to him that Joseph might be Marglewski's informant. After all, the man hung around with the peasants, and a village had no secrets. Besides, he worked on Marglewski's ward, and the skeletal doctor might have taken him into his confidence in that acid way of his. But what could Joseph have to do with the London government? It made no sense; the details did not fit together into any sort of structure. Stefan again felt the urge to warn Woch. But every time he imagined an actual conversation with the operator, he lost his nerve.

In the meantime, something new was happening in the hospital. The apartment next to Stefan's room, previously empty, was to receive a new occupant in the person of Professor Romuald Łądkowski, a former university dean. This scholar, known far beyond the borders of Poland for his research in electroencephalography, had headed his university's psychiatric clinic for eight years before being ousted by the Germans. Now he was coming—unofficially—to the asylum as Pajączkowski's guest. The director himself had driven to the station several times, serving as guard of honor for successive shipments of the professor's baggage. Łądkowski was due in two days. Joseph flew up and down the stairs, gasping for breath, carrying a ladder, a rod, a worn carpet.

All day long, Stefan could hear, through the wall, hammering, the scraping of heavy trunks, and the bumping of furniture. The other doctors greeted Łądkowski's impending arrival with indifference. During dinner silence reigned, highlighted by the furious buzzing of flies. Stefan hung a sheet of wet gauze in his window in an effort to cool the hot dry air. He lay on the bed with a psychology text, looking at people's photographs, keenly aware that they were variants of the same type, their mass existence seeming to clash with his sense of his own unexampled uniqueness. Simple alterations in the basic proportions accounted for individual differences: one face was centered on the eyes, another on the jaw, while the cheeks dominated a third. When he had lived in town, Stefan loved to imagine the faces of people walking ahead of him, especially women. The streets—those moving collections of faces—allowed him to play his game.

Pajączkowski suddenly interrupted these ruminations. He asked what his "respected colleague" was reading and then launched into his favorite topic. "Well, you won't see that anymore," he said, sounding melancholy. "Unfortunately, one no longer encounters such great, classic hysterical attacks with *l'arc de cercle*. I remember, at Charcot's in Paris . . ."

He was getting worked up.

He must have noticed the faint grimace on Stefan's lips, for he added, "Well, in some sense I suppose it's a good thing, though hysteria is still with us. The trend has simply shifted to . . . to . . . but what did I want to tell you?"

Stefan had been waiting for this explanation, since the visit surely heralded something exceptional. Pajpak said that the famous Łądkowski, the friend of the Americans Lashley and Goldschmidt, had been thrown into the street by the Germans. "Into the street," he repeated, his voice breaking. "And in return we must do anything in our power . . ."

He asked Stefan to call on the dean when his turn came.

On the evening of the dean's arrival, Marglewski accompanied Pajączkowski and Kauters on what he called a presentation of letters of accreditation. They three were the highest ranking. Nosilewski and Rygier went on the second day. Staszek and Stefan had their turn on the third. Staszek muttered something about antediluvian customs: they were supposed to be colleagues, working together, united against the enemy, yet when it came to these idiotic visits they had to line up according to their position.

Stefan dug an ancient black tie out of the bottom of his suitcase and put it on, hiding the stains under his jacket. They set out.

Łądkowski looked like a skinny lion with no neck. He had a knobby head, thick silver hair, a nose like a cauliflower with tufts of hair sticking out of the nostrils, and a face of sharp, irregular angles with lopsided gray eyebrows that wavered with his every move. Wrinkles ran down from his carefully shaved chin. His profile suggested Socrates—up to a point.

Having seen several doctors' apartments in the building, Stefan was curious about the professor's, however hastily equipped it may have been. After all, the wagon had made six trips to the station and back.

130

Shelves sagging under masses of books ran along the walls. Most of the books had black bindings with gold letters on the spines. Large folios of professional journals occupied the lower levels. A yellow or green volume shined here and there, as if to break up the monotony. The desk stood catty-corner under the window, a row of textbooks along its front edge. Carpets softened the harshness of what would otherwise have resembled a monk's cell: one, having a deep pile, lay just inside the door; another hung on the wall as a tapestry, forming a background for Ładkowski's silhouette.

Staszek and Stefan muttered obsequiously as they introduced themselves. The professor's conversation was lively: while seeming to talk about everything, in fact he said nothing. The suggestion was that they had come to him for advice and enlightenment. He asked them about their work and their interests—professional interests, of course, personal relations in the asylum being conspicuously unmentioned. He behaved with simple, genuine equality. It was exactly this that put them at a great distance. A kind of noblesse prevented him from subduing his inner haughtiness. Stefan felt even smaller when he looked at two bronze heads standing at opposite ends of a low shelf: Kant and a Neanderthal. He noticed with surprise that although the Neanderthal's bulbous skull and vaulted eye sockets hinted at a wildness absent from the other figure, both heads shared a weary loneliness, as though they embodied the life and death of entire generations.

Portraits hung on the walls: Lister, a Byronic pathos in his forsaken gaze; Pavlov, his jutting chin highlighting the brutal features of an inquisitive child; and Emil Roux, an old man racked by insomnia.

When he judged that he had given the youngsters their due, the professor initiated an exchange of bows and brief but warm handshakes with such breathtaking tact that Stefan and

Staszek, slightly frustrated, found themselves in the corridor almost despite themselves.

"Damn," Stefan reflected, "a great man!" He was suddenly overcome by a desire for one of those elemental discussions that shake the world's foundations, but his friend let him down. The grace Staszek had shown with Ladkowski was gone. During their visit, it seemed as if he had left his troubles outside the professor's door. Now he picked them up again. He was ill with Nosilewska worse than ever. But she, tanned and indifferent, answered his tragic questing gaze with a meaningless smile. She was ever the doctor, seeing a blush as a rush of blood to the face and a thumping heart as a symptom of pressure from the stomach. She was a charged battery of femininity, and her every movement tortured Staszek. Yet he dared not speak: silence afforded him the shreds of hope inherent in uncertainty. Stefan had long acted as comforter, serving so conscientiously that he sometimes savored his own skills. Now and then he struck a false note, bursting into raucous laughter at one of Staszek's confidences or slapping his friend heartily on the back, but he always apologized immediately afterward.

July raced by. August was hot, and apples dropped in the starry darkness. One night, after an evening storm, as trees shaken by thunder settled into stillness in a dusk heavy with moisture, Marglewski appeared ceremoniously in Stefan's room: he was organizing a scientific meeting and a show of patients.

"It will be fascinating," he said. "But I don't want to anticipate. You'll see for yourself."

That very evening Stefan had invited Nosilewska to his room—an attempt to resolve Staszek's unbearable indecision once and for all. His scheme had misfired again.

Rows of plush red chairs had been set up in the library. Rygier entered first, followed by Kauters, Pajączkowski, Nosilewska, and finally Staszek. When it seemed time to start and everyone watched expectantly as Marglewski, standing behind a high lectern covered with papers, cleared his throat, Łądkowski arrived. That was a real surprise. The old man bowed at the doorway, sank into the large armchair Marglewski had prepared for him nearest the podium, crossed his arms over his chest, and sat motionless. Stefan tried to compensate Staszek for his disappointment by maneuvering the chairs so that Nosilewska sat between him and his friend. The lecturer stood behind the lectern, coughed again, and, having arranged his papers, swept the audience with the gleam of his steel-rimmed glasses.

This presentation, he explained, was actually an airing of materials that had not yet been worked up into their final form. Its theme was the specific influences exerted on the human mind by various mental diseases. He spoke of a phenomenon that could be described as the yearning of a convalescent patient for his former malady. It occurred especially among simple, unintelligent people whose inner life schizophrenia had enriched with states of ecstasy. Once cured, such patients mourned their disease.

Marglewski spoke with a discreet, sardonic smile, constantly folding and unfolding his hands. He grew more animated as he got into his subject, rustling his papers, sprinkling his phrases with Latin, building enormous sentences without glancing at his notes. Stefan observed with interest the lovely line of the thighs of Nosilewska's crossed legs. He lost track of Marglewski's deductions, surrendering instead to the rising and falling cadences of his voice. Suddenly the lecturer stepped back from the podium.

"Now, colleagues, I shall demonstrate how what I have called the mourning for his disease can be manifested in a

133

convalescent patient. If you please!" He turned sharply to the open side door. An old man in a cherry-colored hospital robe came in. The white gown of a nurse waiting in the corridor could be seen outside the door.

"Come in, please," said Marglewski with a poor attempt at amiability. "What's your name?"

"Wincenty Łuka."

"How long have you been in the hospital?"

"A long time, a very long time. A year, maybe. At least a year."

"What was the problem?"

"What problem?"

"What brought you to the hospital?" asked Marglewski, holding his impatience in check. Stefan felt bad watching the scene. It was plain that Marglewski cared nothing for the man. All he wanted was to get the statements he needed out of him.

"My son brought me."

The old man suddenly looked confused and lowered his eyes. When he raised them again, they had changed. Marglewski licked his lips and craned forward avidly, his eyes fixed on the patient's sallow face. At the same time he made a brief, significant gesture to the audience, like a conductor holding the rest of the orchestra while evoking a pure solo from a single instrument.

"My son brought me," the old man said in a more assured voice, "because I was seeing things."

"What things?"

The old man waved his hands. His Adam's apple bobbed twice in his dry neck. He was obviously trying to speak. He raised his hands several times, but no words came, and he did not complete the gesture.

"Things," he finally repeated helplessly. "Things."

"Were they beautiful?"

"Beautiful."

"Tell us what it was you saw. Angels? The Lord God? The Blessed Virgin?" Marglewski asked in a matter-of-fact tone.

"No, no," the old man interrupted. He looked at his own pale hands and said, quietly and slowly, "I'm an uneducated man. I don't know how to . . . It started one day when I went out to mow hay, over near Rusiak's farm. That was where it happened. All the trees in the orchard, and the barn, sir, they changed somehow."

"Be more precise. What happened?"

"Everything around Rusiak's farmyard. It was the same, only different."

Marglewski turned quickly to the audience. Rapidly and distinctly, like an actor delivering an aside, he said, "Here we have a schizophrenic suffering disintegration of personality functions—but completely cured."

He intended to go on, but the old man interrupted: "I saw, I saw so much."

He moaned. Beads of sweat appeared on his forehead. He tried to smooth a recalcitrant curl back onto his head.

"Good, very good. We know that. But you don't see things anymore, do you?"

The patient looked down.

"Well?"

"No, I don't," he admitted, and seemed to grow slightly smaller.

"Please observe!" Marglewski addressed the audience. He went up to the old man and spoke to him slowly and emphatically, enunciating carefully. "You will not see things anymore. You are cured. You will go home now, because you don't need us. Nothing is bothering you. Do you understand? You will go home to your son, to your family."

"I won't see things?" the old man repeated, standing motionless.

"No. You are cured."

135

The old man in the cherry robe looked distressed—so distressed that Marglewski beamed, taking a step backward so he would not block the audience's view, pointing surreptitiously at the old man.

The patient walked heavily to the podium. He put his square hands, pale from his stay in the asylum, on the stand.

"Gentlemen," he said in a thin, pained voice. "Why do you have to do this to me? I've already . . . you can put me anywhere, even give me those electric shocks, only please let me stay. We're so poor on the farm, my son has four mouths to feed, what am I supposed to do? If I could work—but my hands and my feet won't listen. I don't have much time left, and I'll eat anything you give me, only let me stay. Please let me stay."

Marglewski's face went through a gamut of emotions as the man spoke. Satisfaction gave way to surprise, then to anxiety, and finally to anger. He gestured to the male nurse, who entered quickly and took the old man by the elbow. At first the patient jerked away like a free man, but then he sagged and let himself be led away unresisting.

Silence filled the room. Marglewski, white as a sheet, pushed his glasses back onto his nose with both hands and returned to the podium with a raucous squeaking of his new shoes. He opened his mouth to speak when Kauters commented from a seat in the back, "Well, there was mourning all right, but not so much for his disease as for three square meals a day."

"Please save your remarks for the end," snapped Marglewski. "I haven't finished. That patient, respected colleagues, has experienced ecstatic states and intense feelings which he is now unable to recount. Before the onset of disease, he was subnormal, almost a cretin. I cured him. But, as they say, you can't teach an old dog new tricks. What you saw just now was the cunning often exhibited by cretins. I have ob-

136

served the symptoms of his mourning for his disease for some time now."

He went on and on in the same vein. Finally he wiped his glasses with a trembling hand, ran his tongue over his lips, rocked back on his heels, and announced, "Well, that's all. Thank you, colleagues."

The ex-dean left immediately. Stefan looked at his watch, leaned toward Nosilewska, and invited her to his room. She was surprised—"Isn't it too late?"—but consented in the end.

As they left, they passed the other doctors gathered outside the door. Marglewski was perorating, holding Rygier by the lapel. Kauters stood silently biting his nails.

Back in his room, Stefan seated Nosilewska alongside Staszek, uncorked a bottle of wine, laid some crackers on a plate, and looked for the orange vodka Aunt Skoczyńska had sent him. After one round, he suddenly remembered something he absolutely had to check on in the third ward, cleared his throat, excused himself, and left with the feeling of having done what he was supposed to do.

He wandered in the corridors, thought about going to see Sekułowski, until Joseph caught him standing at a window. "Doctor, oh, it's a good thing you're here. Paścikowiak—you know, in seventeen—is acting up."

Joseph had his own terminology. If a patient was getting restless, he was "misbehaving." "Acting up" meant something more serious.

Stefan went into the ward.

About a dozen patients watched with mild interest as a man in a bathrobe jumped up and down like a frog, emitting menacing screams that frightened no one, clenching his teeth and waving his arms and legs. Finally he fell onto a bed and began tearing at the sheets.

"Paścikowiak, what's all this?" Stefan began jovially. "Such

137

a peaceful, civilized man, and all of a sudden you start raising hell?"

The deranged man peered out from under his eyebrows. He was short and thin, with the fingers and skull of a hunchback, but without the hump. "Oh, you're on duty today, doctor?" he murmured with embarrassment. "I thought it was Doctor Rygier. I'm sorry, I won't do it again."

Stefan, who disliked Rygier, smiled and asked, "What do you have against Doctor Rygier?"

"Well, just . . . I won't do it again. If you're on duty, doctor, not a peep."

"I'm not on duty. I just happened to be passing by," Stefan said. But that sounded a little too informal, so he corrected himself: "Come on, no more fooling around. Doctor Rygier or me, it's all the same. Otherwise they'll send you right to electroshock."

Paścikowiak sat on the bed, covering the hole in the sheet, and showed his narrow teeth in a silly smile. The records said he was subnormal, but his cleverness did not fit into any diagnostic pigeonhole.

On his way out, Stefan glanced into the next ward. An idiot, a longtime hospital resident, lay murmuring on the nearest bed, covered with a blanket. A few patients were sitting nearby, and one was walking around his bed.

Stefan went in.

"What's going on?" he asked the man who was murmuring. A beggar's face with a red beard, yellowish eyes, and a toothless mouth peeked out from under the blanket. "All right, how much is a hundred and thirteen thousand two hundred and five times twenty-eight thousand six hundred and thirty?"

This was an act of kindness: now the crouched figure murmured in a different tone, fervently, almost prayerfully. A moment later he jabbered, ". . . illion . . . forty-one million . . . ifty-nine thousand . . . dred and fifty."

138

Stefan did not have to check. He knew that the man could multiply and divide six-digit numbers in seconds. When he first arrived at the asylum, Stefan had asked the patient how he did it. The reply was an irate mutter. Once, tempted by Stefan's offer of a piece of chocolate, the idiot promised to tell his secret. Stammering and drooling on the chocolate, he said, "I've got . . . drawers in my head. Click, click. Thousands here, millions here, click click. Snap. And there it is."

"There what is?" asked Stefan, disappointed.

Now the mathematician lowered the blanket, and his face beamed. He was big. "Pump me up!" he lisped.

That meant that he wanted to be given two large numbers.

"Well . . ." Stefan scrupulously counted out the thousands and told him to multiply. The idiot drooled, whispered, hiccuped, and gave the answer. Stefan stood at the foot of the bed, thinking.

The idiot was silent for a moment, then pleaded again, "Pump me up!"

Stefan recited another pair of numbers. Was this what the idiot mathematician needed to be reassured of his own worth? There were times when Stefan felt a sudden fear, as if he should fall to his knees and beg everyone to forgive him for being so normal, for sometimes feeling self-satisfied, for forgetting about them.

He had nowhere to go. In the end he went to see Sekułowski.

The poet was shaving. Noticing a volume of Bernanos on the table, Stefan started to say something about Christian ethics, but Sekułowski did not give him a chance. Standing at the mirror, his face lathered, he shook the shaving brush several times, sending suds flying across the room.

"Doctor, it makes no sense. The church, that old terrorist organization, has been acquiring souls for two thousand years now, and what has come of it? Salvation for some, symptoms for others."

139

Sekułowski was more interested in the problem of genius. Stefan supposed that he thought of it "from the inside," regarding himself as a genius.

"Well, then take van Gogh or Pascal. It's an old story. On the other hand, you garbagemen of the soul know nothing about us."

(Aha! thought Stefan.)

"I remember, from the days of my apprenticeship, a few interesting, pure forms nourished by various literary circles. There was this young writer. Things came easy to him. He had his picture in the papers, interviews, translations, reprints. I was green with envy. I could savor hatred the way the Buddha savored nothingness. Once we ran into each other when both of us were drunk. All his inhibitions were gone. He broke down crying, told me that he envied me my elitism and my high standards. That I had been so protective of what I wrote. That my solitude was so productive and proud. The next day we weren't talking to each other anymore. Soon after, he published an essay on my poems: 'An Abortion Signifying Nothing.' A masterpiece of applied sadism. If you want to listen, please come into the bathroom because I'm going to take a shower."

Lately Sekułowski had been admitting Stefan to his evening ablutions, perhaps as a new way of humiliating him.

He climbed naked into the shower and went on talking. "When I started, I had doubts when my friends praised me. When they didn't, I thought: Aha! And when they started giving out advice—that I was in a rut, a blind alley, that I was burning myself out—then I knew I was on the right track."

He ran a washcloth over his hairy backside.

"There were a couple of old men back then. The first was supposed to be an epic poet—he had never published a single epic, but that was his reputation. They believed in him, but I didn't. He collected mottoes like butterflies. Said he needed them for his 'life's work.' He had been writing this life's work since his youth, constantly correcting it and comparing it to Flaubert's manuscripts. Forever making changes and never getting it right. He would put down three words a week. When he died, somebody lent me his manuscript for a couple of days. Well, not to put too fine a point on it: fluff. Nothing that would last, no effort, no desire. Never trust blowhards—you have to have talent. Don't tell me about Flaubert's endlessly worked-over manuscripts, because I've seen Wilde's work. That's right, Oscar. Did you know that he wrote *The Picture of Dorian Gray* in two weeks?"

He stuck his head under the shower and blew his nose thunderously.

"The other one was famous *in partibus infidelium.* A member of the PEN Club. He read the Upanishads in the original and could write as fluently in French as in Polish. Even the critics respected him. He feared me alone, and hated me because I knew his limits. I could sense them like a hollow bottom in everything he wrote. He would get off to a great start, establish the situation, inject life into the characters, and the action would roll along, until he got to the point where he had to rise above the level of merely putting things down on paper, to step beyond stupidity. But he couldn't do it. That was as far as he could go. Nobody else could hear the false note, so he thought of himself like that naked emperor in Hans Christian Andersen. Do you understand? For me, someone else's writing is like a weight on the floor. All I have to do is walk up to it and decide whether I can pick it up or not. In other words, could I do better or not?"

"And could you?"

Sekułowski scratched his soapy back luxuriantly.

"Almost always. Every so often, when the waves receded,

141

I'd read what I'd written—with some admiration. It's mostly a question of style. The difference in generations comes down to this: once they used to write, 'the dawn smelled of roses.' Then a new wave comes, and for a while they write, 'the morning smelled of piss.' But the device is the same. That's not reform. That's not innovation."

He barked like a seal under the hot stream of water.

"All writing has to have a skeleton, like a woman, but not one you can feel. Also like a woman. Wait a second—I just remembered a great story. Yesterday, Doctor Rygier lent me a couple of old literary journals. What a riot! That pack of critics uttering each word convinced that history was speaking through their mouths, when at best it was yesterday's vodka. Ouch!" His hair had gotten tangled.

He rubbed his belly and went on, "I have a particularly painful memory from that period, on which fate has poured balm. I'll leave names out of it. May he rest peacefully in his grave, upon which I relieve myself," Sekułowski said with a vulgar laugh that may have had something to do with his own nakedness.

He rinsed himself off, reached for his bathrobe, and said calmly, "I pretended to be the most impudent man alive, but actually it was only uncertainty. That's when you pick an ideology like choosing a tie off the rack—whichever seems most colorful and expensive. I was the most defenseless nobody, and above us all, like the brightest of stars, shined a certain critic of the older generation. He wrote like Hafiz praising the locomotive. He was the nineteenth century incarnate. He couldn't breathe in our atmosphere, he could see no one of greatness. He had not yet noticed us, the young. Individually, we didn't matter; if there were ten of us, he'd say good morning. He was a curious type, doctor, a born writer. He had talent, an apt metaphor for every occasion, and humor—and

142

he was completely merciless. For one good metaphor, he was willing to annihilate a book and its author. And did he do it honestly? Don't be naive." Sekułowski combed his wet hair with great attention. "Today I'm absolutely sure that he believed in nothing. Why should he? He was like a beautiful watch missing one tiny screw, a writer with no counterweight. He wasn't foolish enough to become the Polish Conrad, but there was no remedy for that."

He put on his shirt.

"At the time, I had lost God. I don't mean I stopped believing—I lost Him the way some men lose women, for no reason and with no hope of recovery. I suffered, because I needed an oracle. Well, it wouldn't have taken much for that critic to finish me off. But he did believe in one thing. Himself. He oozed that belief the way some women ooze sex. Besides which, he was so famous that he was always right. He read a couple of poems that I sent him, and passed judgment. We were about as much alike as the sun and a shovel"—he laughed, knotting his tie—"and I was a dirty shovel. He talked in terms of first causes, fumbled around, and finally explained to me why my poems were worthless. He hesitated for a while, but in the end he let me go on writing. He let me, do you understand?" Sekułowski made an ugly face. "Well, it's an old story. But when I think that today his name is meaningless to the young, I'm delighted. It's revenge and I didn't even have to lift a finger. It was prepared by life itself. It ripened slowly like a fruit—I know of nothing sweeter," said the poet with great satisfaction, tying the silver belt of his camel smoking jacket.

"Can his contemporaries ever judge a man of genius? Is the van Gogh story fated to be repeated forever?"

"How should I know? Come into the room; it's so humid in here, you could suffocate."

143

"I think that more than one lunatic is an undiscovered genius. Just missing a counterweight, as you put it. Like Morek, for instance." Stefan told him about the idiot mathematician. Sekułowski cut him off angrily: "Morek is as much a genius as your Pajączkowski, but without such a good job."

"Be that as it may, Pajączkowski has a doctorate in psychiatry . . . his work on manic-depression," said Stefan, upset.

"Sure. Most academics are exactly like that mathematician. Maybe they don't drool, but they can't see anything outside their own fields. I knew a lichenologist once. You might not know what that is," he added unexpectedly.

"I do," retorted Stefan, who in fact did not.

"A lichenologist is a specialist in mosses," Sekułowski explained. "This tow-headed scarecrow knew enough Latin to classify, enough physiology to write articles, and enough politics to carry on a conversation with the janitor. But if the discussion turned to fungus, he was lost. This world is crawling with idiot mathematicians. If they cultivate their poor skills in a socially useful direction, they're tolerated. Literature is full of writers who are read by washerwomen but worry over their style with an eye to a posthumous edition of their letters. And what about doctors?"

Stefan tried to steer clear of the sensitive issue of medical practice, hoping to draw some more interesting formulations out of Sekułowski, but all he got was an invitation to kiss his ass. He went upstairs angry. All he knows is how to insult me, he thought.

Stefan decided to eavesdrop at his own door. The corridor was dark and empty as he approached on tiptoe. Silence. A rustling—her dress? The sheets? Then a sound like the plunger being pulled from a syringe. A slap. Then total silence, broken by sobbing. Yes, somebody was definitely crying. Nosilewska? He could not imagine that. He tapped the door lightly, and when no one answered, he knocked once and entered.

144

All the lights were out except the small lamp on the night-stand, which filled the room with a pale-lemon glow that reflected off the mirror to the wall and the bed. The bottle of orange vodka was half-empty: a good sign. The bed looked like a tornado had hit it, but where was Nosilewska? Staszek was lying there alone, in his clothes, his face buried in the pillow. He was crying.

"Staszek, what happened? Where is she?" asked Stefan, rushing to the bed.

Staszek only groaned more loudly.

"Tell me. Come on, what happened?"

Staszek raised his wet, red, snotty face: the emblem of dispair.

"If you . . . If I can . . . If you have . . ."

"Come on, tell me,"

"I won't. If you feel any friendship for me at all, you'll never ask me about it."

"But what happened?" Stefan demanded, curiosity overcoming discretion.

"I feel miserable," moaned Staszek.

Then suddenly he shouted: "I won't tell you! Don't talk to me!" And he ran out, holding the pillow to his chest.

"Give me back my pillow, you maniac!" Stefan shouted after him, but Staszek's footsteps were already thumping down the stairs.

Stefan sat in the armchair, looked around, even lifted the covers and smelled the sheets, but he found out nothing. He was so curious that he wanted to go see Nosilewska, but he restrained himself. Maybe Staszek would calm down by morning. Maybe she would give something away, he thought, but he knew there was little chance of that.

145

Father and Son

It was late September. Heaps of manure were turning black like great molehills in the plowed fields. The aspen near Stefan's window was diseased: dark spots covered its prematurely yellowing leaves. He sat motionless, watching the horizon sharp as a knife. He would sink into a torpor for hours on end, his eyes fixed on the sky, following the patterns of motes dancing in the empty light of the window.

Nosilewska asked him to write a report on a new patient. He agreed eagerly—anything to fill the time.

The patient was one of those slender androgynous girls who padded their busts with lace pillows to transfix men. But the whole beauty of this eighteen-year-old schizophrenic lay in her dark, quick gaze. Her hands fluttered near her face like small doves, lighting on her cheek or under her chin. Once she stopped looking at you, the spell was broken.

The obligation of calling on her became a pleasure for Stefan. The more he fought it, the more he liked her. After a tragic, unfortunate love affair (he was unable to find out exactly what had happened), she yearned to escape from the evil world that had hurt her, to escape into the mirror. She longed to live in her own reflection.

She approached Stefan willingly, knowing that he carried a small nickel mirror. He let her look.

"It's so . . . so marvelous there," she whispered, ceaselessly adjusting her eyelashes, her wavy hair. She could not take her eyes off the gleaming surface.

She reminded Stefan of a couple of other women he knew, the wives of friends in the city. They could sit in front of the mirror all day long, arranging their faces into every possible smile, investigating the sparkle of their eyes, peering at every freckle, every line, smoothing here and pushing there, like alchemists waiting for gold to precipitate in the alembic. The most obvious kind of abnormal obsession, and he had never thought of it before. Birdbrains, of course, but it was a mistake to assume that all neurasthenics were intelligent.

Neurotics could be idiots too, he thought, angry because it sounded almost like an admission: That's what I am.

The girl would often sit in the bathroom, because there was a mirror there. Driven out, she would hang around near the door, stretch her hands out, and beg everyone who opened it to let her look at her own reflection. She tried to see herself in all the chrome fittings.

For some time Stefan had been suffering from insomnia. He would lie in bed reading, waiting for sleep, but it never seemed to come, and when it finally did, he thought he could feel someone standing motionless in the dark room. He knew there was no one, but he would wake up. Only when the first birdsong greeted the dawn could he doze off.

On the night of September 29, the sky sparkling with stars, he fell asleep earlier than usual. But he woke up terrified. A bright light flashed in the window. He got up in his underwear and looked out. Two big cars painted in irregular-shaped patches growled on the winding road, illuminated by the glare of their own headlights reflected off the hospital wall. Germans in dark helmets stood near the door. Several officers came out from under the small roof over the entrance. One of them shouted something. The motors roared, the officers got in, and soldiers jumped onto the running boards. The headlights swept the flower beds, and for an instant the beams of the second car fell on the one ahead. They lit up the passengers' heads, and Stefan saw one bare head among the helmets. He recognized it. The headlights glared against the main gate, where the porter stood blinded, cap in hand. Then the motors roared louder as the cars turned onto the road. On a curve, the headlights picked out a clump of trees, a wreath of leaves, a trunk, and finally the white spine of a birch. Then it was quiet again, the chirping of crickets like a pulse in an enormous ear. Stefan grabbed his coat off the hook, squirmed into it unthinkingly, and ran barefoot down the hall.

All the doctors were gathered on the second floor, and the crossfire of questions was so chaotic that it seemed impossible to understand. The story emerged gradually. The soldiers were from an SS patrol group now stationed at Owsiany. They had arrested a worker at the electricity substation and were looking for others. Marglewski said loudly that no one should go into the woods, because the SS were searching the area, and there was no joking with them.

The soldiers had not searched the hospital, just walked through the wards and talked to Pajączkowski. "The officer had a riding crop, and he struck the table in front of me," said Pajączkowski, pale, his eyes wide. Everyone gradually drifted away as the excitement died down. As he passed Stefan, Marglewski stopped as if to say something, but only nodded maliciously and disappeared down the corridor.

148

Stefan lay awake until morning. He was upset; he kept closing his eyes and reliving the brief nocturnal scene again and again. He could no longer pretend, as he had at first, that the man arrested was someone other than Woch. That large, square head was unmistakable. He groaned under the burden of responsibility he felt. He had to tell someone, had to confess the guilt that was tormenting him, so he went to see Sekułowski. It was early morning.

But the poet would not let him open his mouth. "Can't you see I'm writing? What do you want from me? What am I supposed to do? 'Take a stand' again? Everyone does what he can. What a poet does is suffer beautifully. What about you? Are you waiting for the war to end so every Achilles in the woods can become a Cato? You're as bad as the Furies— at least they make sense, they're women! Leave me alone for a change!"

Brushed off, Stefan thought as he left. He wondered if it would do any good to go take a look at the substation. If there was still electricity in the hospital, somebody had to be working there. And that someone might know what had happened to Woch.

Seeking shelter from his own thoughts, Stefan walked to the farthest corner of the men's ward. Some red spots on the floor caught his eye, but as he came closer, he saw that they were not blood.

A young schizophrenic was making a statue out of clay. Stefan watched him for a long time. The boy's face betrayed nothing. His profile was sharply cut, yellowish, and slightly crooked, like a mobile mask. Sometimes he would close his eyes so peacefully that his eyelashes did not move, and raise his head as his fingertips fluttered like sparrows over the surface of the clay. There was a serenity to his downturned mouth. The demons had stopped tormenting him, sentences died on his lips, he could no longer communicate with strangers: he

149

was absent. That supreme indifference which exists only in crowds or among the unconscious enabled the boy to work in solitude, as if he were in a desert. A tall angel rose from the mound of clay on the round table before him. Its wings, wide as a stricken bird's, were somehow threatening. The long gothic face was beautiful and composed. The hands, held low as if in fear, were wringing a small child's neck.

"What's it called?" asked Stefan.

The boy did not answer. He wiped clay from his fingertips. Joseph spoke up from the corner: a patient was supposed to answer when a doctor talked to him.

"Go ahead and tell the doctor," said Joseph, stepping heavily forward.

Joseph never backed down with patients—they got out of his way. But this boy did not move.

"I know you can talk. Say something or I'll take care of that doll for you." He moved as if he was going to tip the figure over. The boy did not flinch.

"No," said Stefan, confused. "There's no need for that. Joseph, please go to the supply room and fetch a tray of syringes and two ampules of scophetal. The nurse needs them."

He wanted to make it up to the boy for the humiliation. "You know," he said, "it's very strange and beautiful."

The patient stood with his shoulders hunched, hair sticking to his sweaty forehead. A shadow of contempt gathered under his lower lip.

"I don't understand it, but maybe you'll explain it to me someday," said Stefan, slowly shedding his role of psychiatrist.

The boy stared glassy-eyed at his clay-stained fingers.

Then, helplessly, Stefan extended his hand in the simplest of gestures.

The boy seemed terrified: he moved to the other side of the table and hid his hands behind his back. Ashamed, Stefan

150

looked around to make sure there were no staff members in the room. Then the boy reached out suddenly and awkwardly, almost knocking over the statue, and took hold of Stefan's hand. He let go as if it burned him. Then he turned back to the figure and took no further notice of the doctor.

Joseph came up to Stefan during rounds the next day. "Doctor, do you know what that clay is called?"

"No, what?"

"Strangling Angel."

"What?"

Joseph repeated the name.

"Interesting," said Stefan.

"Very interesting. Besides which, the bastard bites," said Joseph, displaying red marks on his large hand. Stefan was awed. He knew all the orderlies' practiced throws. Their motto was: Break a patient's arm before you let him put a scratch on you. The boy must really have been "acting up." And he must have got a good beating too. Despite innumerable orders and reprimands, the orderlies applied a policy of revenge behind the doctors' backs, and patients who made nuisances of themselves were beaten peasant-style, close-in, with the most deliberately painful blows. They were hit through blankets or in the bath, so no marks would show. Stefan knew all this and wanted to order a strict ban on any mistreatment of the boy, but he could not: his authority did not extend to officially forbidden "methods."

"You know, that boy . . ."

"The one with the angel?"

"Right. Be careful he doesn't get hurt."

Joseph was offended. He said he was careful of all the patients. Stefan took a fifty-złoty note out of his pocket. Joseph softened. He got the point. He was always careful, but now he would be extra-careful.

They were standing in the doorway. Patients wandered

nearby, but they might as well have been unattended. As Joseph unobtrusively put the folded banknote away, a determination that surprised him came over Stefan, and in a voice not his own he asked, "Joseph, you wouldn't happen to know what happened to the man the Germans arrested that night? You know who I mean."

They looked at each other. Stefan's heart pounded. Joseph seemed to be stalling. The flash of interest that had appeared in his eyes was submerged in a servile smile. "The guy missing an ear, who worked on the electricity? Woch? Did you know him, doctor?"

"I knew him," Stefan said, feeling that he was putting himself in Joseph's hands. The effort of carrying on the conversation made him feel faint.

An unctuous smile, more and more explicit, crept across Joseph's stupid-cunning face. His eyes widened. "So you knew him, doctor? They say he wasn't the one keeping that stuff in the hole. They say it was his godson, Antek. Well, who knows? But he was a fox, I'll say that. A fox," he repeated, as if he liked the sound of the word. "He drank with the Germans and made deals with them, until he wouldn't give a normal person the time of day, he thought he was so important. He figured he had the German all wrapped up, but the German is a fox, too, and came at night and took him away like a chicken! Today a car came from Owsiany, and they had to make two trips, there was so much stuff. It was hidden under the coils, packed in crates like merchandise!"

"Did you see it?"

"Me? How would I see it? But other people did. They saw it, and they knew. But Woch didn't realize. Everyone else could see it coming."

"What did they do to him?"

"How should I know? You know the sand pit at Rudzień?

152

Where the lake used to be? If you follow the road through the woods and then go to the right . . . They give you a shovel and tell you to dig a hole and stand over it. Then they get a peasant from the road to come and fill it in. They don't like to dirty their hands."

Even though he had supposed as much—even though he knew it could not have been any other way—Stefan felt such rage, such hatred for Joseph, that he had to close his eyes.

"What about the others?" he asked dully.

"The Pościks? Disappeared like a stone in a lake. Nobody knows anything. They must have escaped into the forest. They won't be found in the swamps and caves. And all because they were stupid, they didn't think ahead. They had something there—all that ammunition." His voice dropped on the last words.

Stefan nodded, turned, and went to his room. With a steady hand he shook out a luminal tablet, thought about it, added another, washed them down with water, and dropped onto his bed with his clothes on.

Late that evening he was awakened by a pounding on the door. It was Joseph with a telegram from Aunt Skoczyńska: Stefan's father was seriously ill and he should come home immediately.

He asked Staszek to take over for him on the ward and had no trouble getting several days' leave from Pajączkowski.

"It'll be all right," the old man croaked as he stroked Stefan's hand warmly. "And as long as you're going anyway, try to find out what the Germans are up to."

"Excuse me?"

"Take a look around, see what people are saying. There's been a lot of bad news lately."

"What do you mean, sir?"

"Oh, nothing, nothing, really."

153

When he went to say good-bye to Sekułowski, Stefan found the poet composing, his hair standing on end as if electrified. His eyes jerked every so often in a strange inward gaze. His sonorous, metallic voice carried into the corridor, and Stefan stood in the door listening:

> My heart is a planet of red termites
> Fleeing in horror down a narrow path
> My body—a plaything of sluts and Stylites—
> Is murdering me. My expiring breath
> O Night, tears away the veil at last
> As that dusky girl with bloody thighs, Death,
> Touches my face, a desolate nest . . .

Stefan went in and the poet stopped. A moment later, Stefan was telling him about the sculptor.

"Strangling Angel?" said Sekułowski. "That's interesting, very interesting." He filled a page with his careful, impassioned script. "Blessed are the meek, for theirs is the kingdom of heaven," he read.

Then he looked at Stefan with twinkling eyes. "Because you've helped me a little, I want to show you something."

He shuffled through the sheets of paper covering his bedspread. "I've been dreaming of writing the history of the world from the point of view of another planetary system. This is a sort of introduction." He began reading from a piece of paper. "It is a festering uterus of suns: the universe. It teems with trillions of stellar eggs. Furious procreation bursting forth in grit and black dust, moving beat by beat, darkness by darkness." He was improvising—there were only a few sentences on the paper.

"Where is this other system?" Stefan could not resist asking.

"Nowhere. That's the whole joke."

"And you believe that?"

Sekułowski held his breath. When his bright eyes looked up, he seemed inspired and beautiful.

"No," he said. "I don't believe it. I know it."

Stefan's journey was a nightmare. The filthy dark railroad car smelling of sour sweat was searched three times for lard or butter. There were police, and wild crowds attacked the doors and windows. He could not maintain his personal dignity in the incredible crush, since he was invisible in the darkness and silence was taken as a sign of surrender. Within an hour he was cursing like a sailor.

The city had changed. The streets had German names now, and jackbooted patrols tramped along the cobblestones. Airplanes with black crosses on the wings appeared above the houses from time to time: the sky was German.

The usual smell of boiled cabbage greeted him as he entered the building, and on the second floor the sweet-rotten smell from the furrier's workshop triggered a complex of memories.

He found it hard to control his emotions when he saw the scratched brown door with the lion's head carved in the transom.

The entrance was full of tinware, shelves, and odds and ends, and the cobwebbed frame of his father's unfinished projects rose to the ceiling like macabre animal prototypes. His mother, as Aunt Skoczyńska immediately told him in a dramatic whisper, had moved to the village a month before, since there wasn't enough money to keep the household going. His aunt embraced him in the open doorway and he fell into the naphthalene abundance of her bosom. She kissed him, cried a little, and pushed him into the dining room for bread with jam and tea.

As she brought out the labeled jars of homemade preserves, she talked about the high cost of fat and about a local lawyer. It was a long time before she finally mentioned his father. But then she launched with satisfaction into a detailed account of the events of the past few months. She painted a picture of a misunderstood, unlucky man of greatness, tormented by kidney and heart disease. She alone had supported the great inventor, distant relative though she was. "Your father," she kept repeating, until Stefan began to suspect her of malice, as though she was accusing Stefan of coldness. But no—apparently she was simply expressing heartfelt sympathy. Years ago she had been beautiful. Stefan had even fallen in love with an old photograph of her that he had stolen from her room. But now accretions of flesh drowned what remained of her looks.

After eating and washing, Stefan was at last admitted to the bedroom.

His aunt played the envoy, scurrying back and forth on tiptoe, her hands rowing at her sides as though she was fighting the air resistance. The atmosphere was charged: the Return of the Prodigal Son, thought Stefan as he entered quietly, at which point the Rembrandtian contours in his mind dissolved.

The first thing that struck him was that his mother's collection of cactus, asparagus, and other plants had been mercilessly crammed into the darkest corner of the room. His father lay in bed with a blanket drawn up to his chin. His lemon-colored hands with their gnarled fingers looked like ugly dead ornaments on the blanket border.

"How are you, Father?" he croaked.

His father said nothing, and Stefan yearned for a pleasant, rapid conclusion to the visit. It flashed through his mind that it would be convenient if his father died right at that moment. Then Stefan would be able to kneel at that pathetic spot at the bedside, say a prayer, and leave. That would make everything so much easier.

But his father did not die. On the contrary, he lifted his head and said in a whisper that turned into a groan, "Stefek, Stefek, Stefek," in disbelief and then in joy.

"Father, I heard you weren't feeling well, and I was so upset," he lied.

"Oh," said his father dismissively. He tried to sit up. He needed help and Stefan found the task terribly awkward. He could feel the bones under his touch, the gaps between his father's ribs just beneath the skin, and the feeble remnants of warmth for which the emaciated, helpless body fought.

"Does it hurt?" he asked with sudden concern.

"Sit on the bed. Sit," his father repeated with some impatience.

Stefan perched obediently on the edge of the bedframe; it was uncomfortable, but also very touching. What could he talk about?

He could remember only one expression on his father's face: a vacant gaze into that other world where his inventions took shape. His hands had always been scratched by wire, burned by acid, or dyed some exotic color. Now all that was gone. The last of life trembled gently in the thick dark veins under his freckled skin.

It was painful for Stefan to see.

"I'm so tired," his father said. "It would be better to just go to sleep and not wake up."

"Father, how can you say that?" Stefan blurted, but at the same time he thought: What else is there for a body like this, for a skull that seems to rattle like the meat in a dried-up walnut? His joints are squeaky hinges, his lungs asthmatic moss, his heart a jammed, leaky pump. The body was a decrepit tenement whose inhabitants feared it would collapse on their heads. Stefan recalled Sekułowski's poem: it was our bodies that murdered us, obeying the only law they knew—not our will, but nature.

157

"Father, would you like to eat something?" he asked uncertainly, disturbed by the lightness of the hand now stroking his own. It sounded so stupid, he felt ashamed.

"I don't eat. I don't need anything now. I wanted to tell you so many things, but now . . . I lie awake all night. I can't even sleep anymore," he complained.

"Well, I'll give you a prescription," said Stefan, reaching into his pocket for his pad. "Who's treating you, Marcinkiewicz?"

"Forget it. Don't bother. Yes, Marcinkiewicz. It doesn't matter now." He burrowed deeper into his pillow. "Stefan, this time comes for everyone. When it really hurts, you wish a vein would burst in the brain at night. It might sound stupid, but I wouldn't want to go all at once. It's better to know what's coming. But this doesn't make sense."

Stroking Stefan's hand, he paused as if confused.

"We didn't know each other well. I never had the time. Now I see that it doesn't make any difference. The ones who hurry and the ones who take their time all end up in the same place. Just don't have any regrets. No regrets."

He fell silent, then added, "Never regret that you're in one place and not another. Or that you could have done something but didn't. Don't believe it. You didn't do it because you couldn't do it. Everything makes sense when it ends. Not before. Always and everywhere, when you come down to it, are the same as never and nowhere. No regrets, remember!"

He was quiet again, breathing more deeply than before.

"That's not what I really wanted to tell you. But my head won't obey me anymore."

"Father, can I get you anything? Are you taking any medicine?"

"They keep sticking me with needles," his father said. "Don't worry about it. You regret the life I led, don't you? Tell me."

158

"But Father."

"It's too late for lying now. You regretted the life I led, and you still do, I know that. There was never time. We were strangers. The thing is, I never wanted to give you up. Obviously, I didn't love you, because that would have been . . . I don't know. Stefan, are you doing all right?"

Now it was Stefan who could not find words.

"I'm not asking if you're happy. You know if you're happy only afterward, when it's over. Man lives by change. Tell me, do you have a girl? Do you plan to get married?"

Something caught in Stefan's throat. Here's a man who's dying, almost a stranger, and he's thinking of me. Would I be able to do that? he wondered, but was unable to answer.

"Say something! You have a girl, then?"

Stefan shook his hanging head. His father's eyes were blue, bloodshot, but most of all tired.

"Well. Advice doesn't help. But let me tell you this. We Trzynieckis need women. That's the way we are. We can't handle things on our own. To live a clean life, a person has to be clean himself. You were always pigheaded—maybe I'm not saying it right, but you never knew how to forgive, and that's everything. You don't need to know anything else. I don't know if you can learn now. But anyway, you don't have to look for beauty or intelligence in a woman. Just tenderness. Feeling. The rest comes by itself. But without tenderness . . ."

He closed his eyes.

"Without tenderness it's worth nothing. And tenderness is so easy."

Then he added in his old, strong voice, "Forget all this if you want. Don't listen to my advice. That's wisdom too. But in that case don't listen to anybody's. Now what did I want to tell you? Oh yes, there are three envelopes in the desk."

Stefan was stunned.

159

"And in the bottom drawer there's a roll of paper with a ribbon around it. That's the blueprint for my pneumomotor. The whole plan. Are you listening? Don't forget. As soon as the Germans leave, take it to Frąckowiak. Someone has to make a model. He'll know how."

"But Dad," said Stefan. "You're talking like you're making a will. You're not feeling that bad, are you?"

"I'm not feeling that good either." He did not want comforting. "That pneumomotor is worth a fortune. Believe me. I know what I'm talking about. So take it. It would be better if you took it right now."

With his neck outstretched he whispered, "Aunt Mela is impossible. Absolutely impossible! I can't trust her any farther than I can throw her. Take it now. I'll give you the key."

He almost fell out of bed reaching for his trousers, draped over the chair. In the pocket they found—under a dirty handkerchief, a roll of wire, and a pair of pliers—a bunch of keys. His father held them up to Stefan's face and looked for a small Wertheim key. He handed it to Stefan, who took it and went to the desk. His father dozed off again.

He woke up when Stefan came back. "Well, did you get it?"

Then he looked at Stefan sharply, as if he had just remembered something. "I was not good to your mother," he finally said. "She doesn't even know that I'm . . . I didn't want to tell her."

And he added, "But you, remember! Remember!"

As Stefan got ready to leave, his father asked, "Will you come back?"

"Of course, Dad. I'm not going away. I just have to go into town to take care of a few things. I'll be back for dinner."

His father fell back on the pillow.

. . .

Doctor Marcinkiewicz had an office of glass and white walls. There was a Solux lamp and three quartz ones, whose presence may have been connected with the resettlement of Jewish doctors in the ghetto. Every third word he said to Stefan was "Doctor," but Stefan felt nevertheless that he was not being taken seriously. Their dislike was mutual. Marcinkiewicz gave Stefan an unadorned description of his father's condition: really just a simple case of angina pectoris, except that the pain was weak and not radiating. The changes in coronary circulation, however, were bad news, as bad as could be. He unrolled an electrocardiogram on the polished desktop and began explaining it, but Stefan interrupted him angrily. Only later did he become polite and ask Marcinkiewicz to take good care of his father. Marcinkiewicz declined Stefan's offer of payment, but so feebly that Stefan put some money on the desk anyway. By the time he left, it had disappeared into the drawer.

When he left the doctor's office, Stefan went to several bookshops, looking for *Gargantua and Pantagruel*. It was an old favorite of his, and now that he had some money, he wanted to buy Boy's translation. But he could not find it anywhere: times were hard for bookshops. He finally got lucky in a secondhand store. Through an old acquaintance he also picked up some textbooks that were sold only to Germans, and got a copy of the latest issue of a German scholarly journal for Pajpak. Since he now had a fairly heavy load, he decided to go home by tram. A grotesquely overcrowded tram stopped; people pressed against the sweaty windows like fish in an aquarium. He grabbed a rail outside the door with his free hand and jumped onto the step. But he felt someone grab his collar from behind and pull him down. He jumped onto the

161

sidewalk to avoid falling, and found himself looking right into the face of a young, smooth-cheeked German who unceremoniously elbowed him out of the way. When Stefan tried to climb up after him, a second German, accompanying the first, pushed him aside even more violently.

"Mein Herr!" Stefan shouted, giving him a shove of his own in return. The second German kicked Stefan in the backside with his polished boot. The bell rang and the car moved off.

Stefan stood on the sidewalk. Several passersby had stopped. He felt terribly confused and walked away, pretending that something across the street had caught his eye. He would not wait for the next tram. The incident left him so depressed that he gave up on his idea of visiting an old friend from school. Instead he walked home through the dry, rustling leaves.

His father was sitting up in bed smacking his lips as he ate curls of scrambled egg from an aluminum pan. Stefan told him what had happened.

"Yes, that's the way they are," his father said. "Volk der Dichter. Well, too bad. You see what their young people are like. Until last September I used to correspond with Volliger—you remember, the firm that was interested in my automatic tie presser. Then they just stopped answering. It's a good thing I didn't send them the plans. They got vulgar and uncivilized. In the end we're all getting vulgar and uncivilized."

He suddenly leaned over and shouted at the top of his lungs, "Melania! Melaniaaa!"

Stefan was amazed, but there was a shuffling of feet and his aunt's face appeared around the door.

"Give me a little more herring, but more onion this time. What about you, Stefan? Something to eat?"

"No." He felt disenchanted. When he left Marcinkiewicz, he had been ready to see his father again, had felt more affectionate, but now the old man had ruined his appetite.

162

"Father, I really have to get back today." He launched into a complex description of the hospital, making it clear that his responsibilities were enormous.

"Be careful, watch yourself," said his father, looking around for a piece of herring that had slipped off his plate. He found it, ate it with a big mouthful of bread, and concluded: "Don't get too wrapped up in things there. I don't know what to think, after what happened in Koluchów."

"What happened?" Stefan asked, recognizing the name.

"Haven't you heard?" asked his father, wiping his plate with bread. "There's an insane asylum there," he said, glancing obliquely at his son to make sure he hadn't offended him.

"Yes, it's a small private hospital. So what happened?"

"The Germans took it over and turned it into a military hospital. All the lunatics—I mean patients—were deported. To the camps, they say."

"What are you talking about?" exclaimed Stefan, incredulous. The latest German treatise on therapy for paranoia, printed since the outbreak of the war, was in his briefcase.

"I don't know, but that's what they say. Oh, Stefan, I forgot! I meant to tell you right away. Uncle Anzelm is angry at us."

"So?" Stefan said. He didn't care.

"He says you've been living right there in Ksawery's backyard for the better part of a year, and you haven't gone to visit him once."

"Then Uncle Ksawery ought to be angry, not Anzelm."

"You know how Anzelm is. Let's not get him going. You could stop in there someday. Ksawery likes you, he really does."

"Fine, Father. I will."

By the time Stefan was ready to leave, his father's mind was on his latest inventions: soy caviar and cutlets made from leaves.

"Chlorophyll is very healthy. Just think, some trees live for six hundred years. There's no meat in them at all, but let me tell you, with my extract these cutlets are delicious. Too bad I ate the last ones yesterday. When that stupid Melania sent you the telegram."

Stefan learned that the telegram had been prompted by a sudden deterioration of relations between his father and his aunt, who had decided to leave. But they made up before Stefan arrived.

"I'll give you a jar of my caviar. You know how it's made? First you boil the soy, then color it with carbon—*carbo animalis*, you know what I mean?—then salt and my extract."

"The same extract as in the cutlets?" asked Stefan, his expression serious.

"Of course not! A different one—special—and you use olive oil for flavor. A Jew was going to get me a whole barrel, but they stuck him in a camp."

Stefan kissed his father's hand and was about to leave.

"Wait, wait, I haven't told you about the cutlets."

The old man is completely senile, thought Stefan, with some tenderness, but without a trace of the morning's emotion.

Stefan went to the station to go back to the asylum. But it was impossible: the crowd and the turmoil were horrendous. People crawled like bugs through the cars, while a bearded giant barricaded in a toilet pulled bulging suitcases in one after another. People even clambered on the roof. Stefan was still not used to traveling that way. He tried in vain to get into the car by explaining that he had to get to Bierzyniec. He was told to run along behind the train. He was ready to give up and go home to his father's when somebody tugged at his sleeve. A stranger in a stained cap and a coat sewn from a plaid blanket. "Are you going to Bierzyniec?"

"Yes."

"You don't have a platzkart?"

"No."

"We can go together, but it'll cost you."

"Fair enough," Stefan said. The stranger disappeared into the crowd and returned a moment later clutching a conductor by the elbow.

"You give him a hundred," he said to Stefan. Stefan paid, and the conductor opened a notebook, adding the banknote to a stack of others. He wet his finger, rubbed his pocket flap, and pulled out a key. They followed him as he crawled under the car to the other side of the train and led them to a tiny compartment. "Have a good trip," said the conductor politely, stroking his mustache and saluting.

"Thanks very much," said Stefan, but his traveling companion suddenly lost interest in him and turned to the window. The man's face was not so much old as desolate, with dark skin and a thin, sunken mouth. When he took off his coat and hung it up, Stefan saw that he had large, heavy hands with fingers that looked as though they were used to gripping angular objects. His fingernails were thick and dark, like pieces of a nutshell. He pulled his cap down over his eyes and sat in the corner. The train began to move. Two more passengers could have fit into their compartment, which did not endear them to the people jammed in the corridor. Their faces were twisted into scowls. Against the glass stood an elegant man with a delicate, plump face that seemed eternally moist. He rattled the handle and knocked loudly several times. Finally he started to shout, and when his voice failed to carry through the glass, he took out a document with a German stamp and pressed it to the glass.

"Open up right now," he roared.

For a while Stefan's companion pretended not to hear anything, then he leaped to his feet and pounded back on the glass: "Shut up! This is a crew compartment, asshole!"

The elegant man mouthed something to save face and withdrew. The rest of the trip passed without incident. When they reached the hills approaching Bierzyniec, the stranger stood up and put on his coat. When its folds bumped the wooden partition, they made a hollow sound as if there was metal inside. The train came around the turn to the empty platform and the brakes shrieked. Stefan and the stranger jumped out as the locomotive rounded the bend, huffing to get up steam for the hill. They slipped through a gap in the iron barrier. A sentimental autumn landscape unfolded behind the station. Stefan blinked up at the sun.

The stranger walked along beside him. They went through the town and turned on to the road that ran through the gorge. The stranger seemed to hesitate for a moment.

"Are you going to the asylum?" Stefan asked, curious.

For a moment the stranger did not reply. Then he said, "No, I just want to get some fresh air."

They walked on for a few hundred meters. At the head of the gorge, where the trees still blocked the view of the little brick building, something occurred to Stefan. "Excuse me," he mumbled, stopping.

The stranger also stopped and looked at him.

"You wouldn't by any chance be going to the substation? Don't say anything, but, well—please don't go there!"

The stranger watched him warily, neither joking nor disbelieving; the grimace of a half-smile was on his lips and his eyes were wide and unblinking. He didn't say anything, but he didn't move either.

"There are Germans there," Stefan said quickly, his voice hushed. "Don't go there. They took Woch away. He was arrested. They probably . . ." He broke off.

"Who are you?" asked the stranger. His face had turned gray as a stone. He put his hand in his pocket, and the hint of a smile that remained on his face became an empty twist of his mouth.

"I'm a doctor at the asylum. I knew him." He could not go on.

"There are German at the substation?" asked the stranger. He spoke like a man carrying a heavy weight. "Well, it's none of my business," he added slowly. He was clearly mulling something over. Then he gave a start and leaned so close that Stefan could feel his breath. "What about the others?"

"The Pościks?" Stefan caught on eagerly. "They got away. The Germans didn't get them. They're in the woods, with the partisans. That's what I heard, anyway."

The stranger looked around, grabbed Stefan's hand and gave it a short painful squeeze, and walked straight ahead.

Before he reached the turn, he climbed the hill alongside the road and disappeared into the trees. Stefan took a deep breath and started up the hill toward the hospital. When he neared the stone arch, he turned his head and looked back, down into the woods, searching for his traveling companion. At first he was fooled by the tree trunks that showed among the bright yellow and reddish leaves. Then he spotted him. The stranger was far away, standing still, black against the background of the landscape. But only for an instant: he vanished among the trees.

Pajączkowski stood before the door of the men's wing, a rare sight in the yard. Father Niezgłoba was with him. The priest had been feeling well for several weeks and could have returned to his pastoral duties, but his substitute from the diocese would be at his parish until the end of the year. Besides, he admitted that he had no desire to spend Christmas with his parishioners.

"It's funny," he said, "but they get angry if you don't have a drink with every one of them. It's the same thing at New

167

Year's, and Easter, with the blessed food, is the worst of all. I'm not supposed to drink now, but you think they care about my health? I'm in no hurry. It's better if I stay here, professor," he told Pajączkowski, "if you don't throw me out."

Pajączkowski had a weakness for the Church. It was only thanks to him that two Sisters of Charity notorious for their merciless treatment of patients had not been dismissed years ago when a ministerial commission came to investigate the death of a patient who had been scalded in the bathtub. Actually, they left a few weeks later, under his covert pressure. At least that was the story.

Now the priest was trying to talk Pajączkowski into letting him hold Mass next Sunday in the little chapel against the north wall of the yard. He had already checked to make sure there would be no problems with the local parish, and he had everything he needed, except for Pajączkowski's permission. The director wanted to go ahead, but was afraid of what his colleagues might say. Everyone knew that Mass in an insane asylum was a circus. It was all right for the staff, but the priest thought that the healthier patients at least would be up to it as well.

Pajączkowski was sweating, but when he finally agreed, he calmed down at once. Then he remembered some pressing business and excused himself.

That was when Stefan arrived. "Well, Father, no more visits from the Princess?" he asked, looking around the unkempt garden. The leaves were falling from the trees on the ridge faster than from those on lower ground. At first Stefan did not realize that he had hurt the priest's feelings.

"My mind, dear doctor, may be compared to a musical instrument with a few strings out of tune. The soul, that marvelous artist, was therefore unable to play the proper melody. But now, since you gentlemen have treated me, I am completely healthy. And grateful."

168

"In other words, Father, you are comparing us to piano-tuners," said Stefan with an inward smile, though he maintained his serious expression. "Perhaps you're right," he went on. "A nineteenth-century theologian is said to have stated that the telodendria, the edges of nerve cells, are immersed in the universal ether—except that physics had already disproved the existence of the ether."

"Not long ago there was a different note in your voice," the priest said sadly. "Please excuse the obsession of a former patient, doctor, but it seems to me that Mr. Sekułowski has acted on you like wormwood. You are naturally good-hearted, but seeing him has given you a bitter streak that, I am sure, is foreign to you."

"Good-hearted?" Stefan laughed. "Me? That is a compliment I have usually been spared, Father."

"I do hope that you will come on Sunday. It only remains for you to give me your recommendation as to which of the patients should be allowed to take part in the Mass. On the one hand I would like as many of them as possible to be there, since it has been so many years, while on the other . . ." He hesitated.

"I understand," said Stefan. "In my view, however, the plan is inadvisable."

"Inadvisable?" The priest was visibly disheartened. "Don't you think that . . ."

"I think there are times when even God could compromise Himself."

The priest looked down. "Indeed. Unfortunately, I know full well that I will be unable to find the right words, because I am just an ordinary village priest. I admit that when I was in school I dreamed of meeting an unbelieving but powerful spirit. So that I could harness it and lead it . . ."

"Harness it? That sounds strange, Father."

"I was thinking of harnessing it with love, but that was a

169

sin. I only realized that later: the sin of pride. Then I discovered that living among people teaches us many other things. I know very well how little I am worth. Every one of you doctors has a whole battery of arguments that could demolish my priestly wisdom."

Stefan was annoyed by the priest's mawkish tone. He looked around.

The patients were walking along the paths to the building; it was dinner time.

"Let's keep this between us," Stefan said, starting to leave. "And you know, Father, our bond of secrecy is as strict as yours, leaving heaven out of it. But tell me something. Have you ever had doubts, Father?"

"What kind of answer do you want, doctor?"

"I would like to hear the truth."

"Forgive me: it seems that you seldom open the Gospels. Please take a look at chapters 27 and 46 of Saint Matthew. More than once, those have been my words."

The priest left. The yard was almost empty. The cherry-colored robes moved so evenly that an unseen force might have been combing them out of the gold-tinged gardens. Last of all came an orderly smoking a cigarette. As Stefan walked past a bare lilac bush, he saw someone crouching behind it. He wanted to call the orderly, but stopped himself. The patient, bent low, was clumsily stroking the silvery grass with a stiff hand.

Acheron

Stefan was coming back from a walk. Fluffy gold filled the roadside ditches, as if Ali Baba's mule had passed, spilling sequins from an open sack. A chestnut tree burned against the gray sky like an abandoned suit of armor. In the distance, the forest seemed to be rusting. As Stefan walked, the leaves thickly layered underfoot were alternately yellow and brown, like musical variations on a red theme. Twilight smoldered orange at the end of the path. Faraway orchards faded against the horizon. Leaves blown into a hissing cloud raced among a herd of tree trunks. Stefan was still dazzled by the colors when he entered the library to pick up a book he had left there.

Pajpak was standing at the telephone on the wall, pressing the receiver so hard that his ear had turned white. He was hardly saying anything, just mumbling, "Yes . . . yes . . . yes." Then he said, "Thank you," and replaced the receiver with both hands.

He stood there, still holding the telephone, and Stefan hurried over.

171

"My dear, dear colleague," Pajączkowski whispered, and Stefan's heart went out to him.

"Are you feeling weak, professor? Do you want some coramin? I'll run to the medicine room."

"No, it's not that. I mean it's not me," the old man mumbled. He stood up straight and guided himself along the wall like a blind man until he reached the window.

The autumn red, laden with the smell of mold and speckled yellow among the leaves, broke against the window like a flood tide.

"It's the end," he said abruptly, then repeated: "The end." He lowered his gray head.

"I'll see the dean. Yes, that's what I'll do. What time is it?"

"Five."

"Then he's sure to be . . . home."

The dean was always home.

Turning as if he had just noticed Stefan, he said, "And you're coming with me."

"What's going on, professor?"

"Nothing so far. And God will not allow it. No, He will not let it happen. But we'll . . . You come with me as a witness. It'll be easier for me that way, safer to talk, because you know how His Excellency is."

A spark of Pajpak's humor shined in his use of the dean's ceremonial title, then disappeared.

Going to a doctor's apartment was one thing, but going to the dean's was another. The door was plain and white, like all the others. Pajączkowski tapped too softly to be heard inside.

He waited and tried again, louder. Stefan was about to knock himself, but the director skittishly pushed him away: You don't know how to do it, you'll screw it up.

"Come in!"

A powerful voice. It was still reverberating as they entered. Stefan had seen the room before, but it looked different in the sunset light. The white walls had taken on a fiery color. It looked like a lion's den. The old gold on the spines of the books seemed like some exotic inlay. The sun tinged the veneer of the sideboard and shelves with a deep mahogany. Pools of light shimmered in the grain of the wood; sparks glinted in the dean's hair. He was behind his desk as always, leaning over a thick book, staring at Pajpak and Stefan.

Pajączkowski stammered through his introduction. He apologized, he knew they were interrupting, but *vis maior*—for the general good. Then he came to the point.

"I just had a telephone call, Excellency, from Kocierba, the pharmacist in Bierzynice. At eight o'clock this morning a company of Germans and Cossack police—Ukrainians—arrived in the village. They were ordered to be silent, but somebody talked. They have come to liquidate our asylum."

Pajpak seemed somehow diminished. Only his crooked nose moved. He was through.

The dean, as befits a man of science, questioned the reliability of the pharmacist's information. Pajączkowski spoke in his defense.

"He is a solid man, Excellency. He has been here for thirty years. He remembers you from the times of the servant Olgierd. You wouldn't know him, because he is a little man"—Pajączkowski measured out a modest height above the floor—"but he is honest."

He took a breath and said, "Excellency, this news is so terrible that I would prefer not to believe it. But it is our—I mean, it is my obligation to believe it." Now came the hardest part of his speech. However humble and unsure of himself, he realized how cold their reception had been: the dean had not even invited them to sit down. Two chairs by the desk

173

stood empty, shadowed in the gold reflection of the setting sun. The dean sat waiting, his large, veined hand resting on his book. This meant that the entire scene was an interlude, an interruption of more important business beyond the ken of his guests.

"I have learned, Excellency, that these soldiers are commanded by a German psychiatrist. In other words, a colleague of ours. A Doctor Thiessdorff."

He paused. The dean was silent. He merely raised his gray eyebrows as if to say: I don't know the name.

"Yes. A young man. Member of the SS. And though I realize what a thankless undertaking it is—what else can we do? We must go see him in Bierzyniec today, Excellency, because tomorrow . . . " His voice failed. "The Germans have notified Mr. Pietrzykowski, the mayor, that they need forty people for a labor detail tomorrow morning."

"This news is not entirely unexpected," the dean said quickly. It was strange that such a big man could speak so quietly. "I have anticipated it, though perhaps not in this form, ever since Rosegger's article. Surely you remember it."

Pajpak nodded vigorously: he remembered, he was listening, he was paying attention.

"I do not know, however, what my role in all this might be," the dean went on. "As far as I know, the staff and the doctors are in no danger. Whereas the patients . . ."

He should not have said that. Accustomed as he was to preparing his words well in advance, he must not have been thinking this time.

Pajączkowski appeared no different, but though his thin hand was still an old man's hand, it did not tremble as it rested on the corner of the desk.

"These are times," he said, "in which human life is losing its value. These are horrible times, but Your Excellency's name should still be able to guard this house like a shield and save the lives of one hundred and eighty unfortunate people."

The dean's other hand, which had remained behind the desk as if not taking part in the discussion, now intruded in a vigorous horizontal gesture where meaning was clear: Silence.

"I am not, after all, the director of this institution," he said. "I am not even listed as an employee. I hold no position here. My presence is entirely unofficial, and I believe that serious problems may arise for me—and for you—on that account. However, I will remain here if you so wish. As for my mediation, the Germans have already evaluated what services I have performed. In Warsaw. And you know to what effect. The wild young Aryan who, as you say, intends to kill our patients tomorrow is following the orders of an authority that respects neither age nor academic reputation."

Silence fell, a change coming slowly over the room. The last rays of the setting sun moved across the cabinet by the window in a red, weeping stain so delicate that Stefan, though riveted by the conversation, could not help following it with his eyes. Then a blue veil dropped over the room like clear water. It got darker, and sadder, the way the lighting announces a new scene in a well-staged play.

"I am going there now," said Pajączkowski, who stood erect and looked quixotic with his small beard. "I thought that you would accompany me."

The dean did not move.

"In that case, I'll be off. Good-bye, Excellency."

They left. In the corridor, Stefan felt very small beside the old man. The tiny, withered face bore a great deal of pride at that moment.

"I'm going now," he said, as they stood at the top of the light-dappled staircase. "I trust you will keep everything you have just heard to yourself until I return."

He put his hand on the rail. "The dean has been going through a difficult time. He was thrown out of the laboratory in which he laid the groundwork for electroencephalography. His work was important not only in Poland. Still, I didn't think . . ." Here a shade of the old Pajpak returned, but only for an instant: his beard trembled. "I don't know. *Acheronta movebo?*"

"You want me to go along?" Stefan suddenly asked. Fear swept over him. He felt stunned, just as he had when the German kicked him, and he took a step back.

"No. What could you do? Only Kauters, perhaps." He added, after a long pause, "But he wouldn't go. I'm sure of that. The scene in there was enough for me."

He started down the empty stone staircase with strides so firm that it was as if he wanted to refute all the rumors of his poor health.

Stefan was still standing at the top of the stairs when Marglewski appeared. The scrawny doctor was in bubbling spirits. He grabbed a button of Stefan's shirt and drew him to the window.

"Have you heard that the priest is saying Mass tomorrow? He needs altar boys and I promised Rygier that I would find some for him. You know who's going to serve? Little Piotr from my ward! You know who I mean?"

Stefan remembered a small blond boy with a face like a Murillo angel and a shock of gold hair. A drooling, retarded cretin.

"It'll be out of this world! Listen, we absolutely have to . . ."

Stefan sacrificed the button, shouted that he was in a hurry, and left Marglewski in mid-sentence. He ran out of the building and down the road to Bierzyniec where Pajączkowski had gone. As he flew downhill, barely seeing the road, he heard a sound above the crunching of the leaves. He stopped and looked up. It was a motor. Someone was driving up the hill. A cloud of dust drew nearer behind the trees. Stefan could not help shivering, as if an icy wind had blown over him. He turned back quickly. He had almost reached the stone arch with its worn inscription when the engine roared past him. He leaned against the pillar.

It was a German military vehicle, a slab-sided Kübelwagen, rocking as it climbed in second gear. The driver's helmet showed dark behind the windshield. The vehicle turned and stopped at the gate with a clatter.

Stefan walked toward it.

A big German was standing at the wall, wearing a camouflage cape, dark goggles pushed up onto his helmet, and black gloves with embroidered labels. Patches of mud were drying on the folds of his cape. He was saying something loudly to the gatekeeper. When Stefan heard his question, he answered in German: "Unfortunately the director is not here at the moment. May I help you?"

"Things have to be straightened out here," the German replied. "Are you the vice-director?"

"I'm a doctor here."

"All right, then. Let's go inside."

The German walked in decisively, as if already familiar with the place. The driver remained behind the wheel. Stefan noticed that he kept his hand on an automatic pistol lying on the seat beside him.

Stefan led the German into the main office.

"How many patients are here at present?"

"I'm sorry, but I don't know if . . ."

"I'll decide when you should apologize," the German said sharply. "Answer me."

"About a hundred and sixty."

177

"I must have the exact figure. Let me see the papers."

"That is confidential."

"Don't give me that shit," answered the German. Stefan took the book off the shelf and opened it. The hospital population was 186.

"So. You're sure you're not lying?"

Stefan's cheeks felt numb. He couldn't take his eyes off the German's sharp chin. His cold, sweaty fingers were clenched into fists. Those washed-out German eyes had seen hundreds of people strip naked at the edges of ditches, making meaningless movements as, understanding nothing, they tried to prepare their living bodies to tumble into the mud. The room spun—only the tall figure with the green cape thrown over his shoulders remained fixed.

"What a disgusting backwater this is," the German said. "Two days hunting down those swine in the woods. A special committee is coming here. If you hide one single patient, that's it." No explicit threat, no gestures, no expression. Yet Stefan still felt numb inside. His lips were dry. He kept licking them.

"Now show me all the buildings."

"Only doctors are allowed in the wards," said Stefan, barely above a whisper. "Those are the rules."

"We make the rules," said the German. "Enough stalling."

He pushed past Stefan, staggering him. They walked across the yard at a brisk pace. The German looked around, asking questions. How many beds in a given ward? How many exits? Are the windows barred? How many patients?

Finally, on his way out, he asked how many staff and doctors there were. He stopped at the broadest stretch of lawn and looked both ways, as if taking its dimensions.

"You can sleep easy," he said when they got back to the vehicle. "Nothing will happen to you. But if we find a bandit here, or a weapon, or anything like that, I wouldn't want to be in your shoes."

178

The vehicle started as the German settled his enormous bulk into the backseat. Only then did Stefan realize two peculiar things: he had seen not a single doctor or nurse, even though they were usually out walking in the evening, and he had no idea who the German was. His cape had covered his insignia. He remembered nothing of his face, just the helmet and dark glasses. The man might as well have been a Martian, Stefan was thinking when the sound of light footsteps ended his reverie.

"What was all that about?" Nosilewska, her eyes more beautiful than usual, stood before him, flushed from excitement and from running. She was not wearing her medical smock. Confused, Stefan explained that he did not know himself—a German had wanted to look around the hospital. Apparently they were scouring the woods for partisans, so he had come here.

He was careful not to mention Pajpak.

Nosilewska had been sent by Rygier and Marglewski, who, though they had watched from an upstairs window as the vehicle left, did not want to come out. Nor had they let her come downstairs earlier: they were playing it safe.

Leaving her rather impolitely, Stefan started back down the path.

He looked at his watch: seven. It would be getting dark soon. The German had spent almost half an hour there. Pajpak should be back soon. Everything seemed strange, alien in the gloom. He looked at the asylum. The dark contours of the buildings rose against clouds which, backlighted by the moon, looked as if they had lamps in them.

He had gone several hundred steps when he heard someone coming toward him through the leaves on the opposite side of the road. It was dark; the clouds obscured the moon. Stefan, guiding himself by sound, crossed the road, and recognized the director only when they were just three steps apart. "There

179

was a German at the hospital, sir," he began, but broke off.

Pajączkowski said nothing. Stefan walked beside him, now a little ahead, now slightly behind. They reached the gate and went to Pajpak's office. "This is it," the professor finally said, unlocking the door and going in. Although they both knew where the furniture was and the switch, they bumped into each other three times before turning on the light. Then Stefan, who had been burning with questions, stepped back in fear.

Pajączkowski looked yellow and parched. His pupils were as wide as buttons.

"Professor," whispered Stefan. And then louder: "Professor."

Pajączkowski walked to the cabinet and took out a small bottle with a worn cork—*spiritus vini concentratus*. He splashed some into a tumbler, because there was no proper glass, drank it, and choked. Then he sat down in an armchair and held his head in his hands.

"The whole way there," he said, "I kept going over what I would say. If he told me the deranged were useless, I was going to appeal to the work of two deranged Germans, Bleuler and Moebius. If he talked about the Nuremberg legislation, I would explain that we were an occupied country and our legal status would not be clarified until a peace treaty was signed. If he demanded that we turn over the incurables, I would say that in medicine there is no such thing as a hopeless case. You never rule out the unknown: that is one of the obligations of a doctor. If he said that this was an enemy country and he was a German, I would remind him that he was a doctor above all else."

"Please, professor," whispered Stefan, pleading.

"Yes, I know you don't want to hear this. When I got there, I don't know if I said three words. I was slapped in the face."

"What?" croaked Stefan.

"The Ukrainian on duty told me that Obersturmführer

180

Hutka had gone to the asylum to check on the population and work out the tactical plan. That's how he put it. I hope you gave false numbers."

"No, I . . . I mean, he saw them himself."

"Yes, I see. Yes, yes."

Pajpak poured himself some bromine with luminal from a second bottle, drank it, and wiped his mouth with the back of his hand. Then he asked Stefan to summon all the doctors to the library.

"The dean too?"

"What? Yes. Well, maybe not. No."

The lights were already on in the library when Stefan entered with Nosilewska and Rygier. Then Kauters, Marglewski, and Staszek appeared. Pajączkowski waited until they were all seated. Tersely and without the usual digressions he announced that the German and Ukrainian unit that had pacified—in other words, burned and slaughtered—the village of Owsiany planned to exterminate the patients of the asylum. The Germans had organized a labor gang for next morning, since they had learned from experience that mental patients—unlike peasants, who would usually dig their own graves—were incapable of organized tasks. He had learned all he needed to know from his attempt to approach Doctor Thiessdorff.

"Barely had I informed him of the purpose of my call when he slapped me. I wanted to believe that he was outraged at my slanderous suggestion of his intentions, but the Ukrainian duty officer informed me that they had already received orders: they are getting extra ammunition today. This duty officer seemed honest enough, if that word has any meaning under the circumstances."

Pajączkowski concluded by explaining the true purpose of Obersturmführer Hutka's afternoon visit.

"I would like you, ladies and gentlemen, to think all this

181

over, to make certain decisions, and take steps. . . . I am the director, but I am simply . . . simply not man enough to . . ."

His voice failed.

"We could release the patients into the woods and let them get away by themselves. There's a local train to Warsaw at two in the morning," Stefan began, but stopped when he met dead silence.

Pajpak shrugged. "I thought of that. But it seems unlikely to work. The patients would be rounded up easily. And they would never survive in the forest anyway. It would be the simplest thing, but it's not a solution."

"I believe," said Marglewski, his tone categorical, "that we have to yield to superior force. Like Archimedes. We should leave, just leave the hospital."

"With the patients?"

"Just leave."

"In other words, escape. That, of course, is one way out," the old man said softly, strangely patient. "The Germans can hit me in the face, throw us out of here, do whatever they like. But I am not just the director of this institution. I am a doctor. As are all of you."

"Nonsense," Marglewski muttered, resting his chin on his hand.

"Haven't you tried . . . any other method?" asked Kauters. Everyone looked at him.

"What do you have in mind?"

"Well, some sort of appeasement."

Pajączkowski finally caught on. "A bribe?"

"When will they be here?"

"Between seven and eight in the morning."

Marglewski, who had been squirming strangely, suddenly pushed his chair back, leaned forward, his hands spread wide

182

on the table, and said, "I regard it as my duty to preserve the scholarly work that is the common property of everyone, not only mine. I see no other course open to me. Farewell, ladies and gentlemen."

Head high, he walked out without looking at anyone.

"Wait a minute!" shouted Staszek.

Pajączkowski made a gesture of helplessness. They all looked at the door.

"So," Pajpak said in a fragile voice. "He works here for twenty years, and now this. I didn't know, I never would have supposed—I, a psychologist, a specialist in personalities . . ."

Then he screamed, "We must not think of ourselves! We must think of them!" He struck the table with his fist, and began to weep, coughing and shaking.

Nosilewska led him to a chair, and he sat down reluctantly. The light struck her hair in golden streaks as she bent over the old man and discreetly held his wrist to check his pulse. She hurried back to her chair.

Suddenly everyone began talking at once.

"It's still not certain."

"I'm going to call the pharmacist."

"In any case we have to hide Sekułowski." (That was Stefan.)

"And the priest too."

"But wasn't he discharged?"

"No, that's the point."

"Well, let's go to the office."

"The Germans have already checked the numbers," said Stefan dully. "And made me—I mean all of us—responsible."

Kauters maintained his silence.

Pajączkowski, now calm, stood up again. His eyes were red. Stefan approached him. "Professor, we have to decide. Some of them must be hidden."

"We must hide all the patients who are conscious," said the director.

"Maybe a few of the more valuable ones could be . . ." Rygier hesitated.

"Perhaps we can let all the convalescents go?"

"They have no papers. They'd be picked up at the station."

"So which ones do we hide?" asked Staszek with nervous boldness.

"I'm telling you, the most valuable ones," Rygier repeated.

"I cannot make decisions about value. Just as long as they don't betray the others," said Pajpak. "That's all."

"So we are supposed to make a selection?"

"Gentlemen, please go to the wards. Doctor Nosilewska, you will want to inform the nursing staff."

Everyone headed for the door. Pajpak stood off to the side, leaning with both hands on the back of a chair. Stefan, the last to leave, heard him whispering.

"Excuse me?" he asked, assuming that Pajączkowski was speaking to him. But the old man did not even hear him.

"They'll be so afraid," he was whispering almost breathlessly.

No one slept that night. The selection yielded dubious results: about twenty patients, but no one could vouch for their nerves. The supposedly secret news somehow spread through the hospital. Young Joseph ran around in an open robe, not leaving Pajączkowski's side.

In the women's ward, a half-naked crowd danced in a blur of limbs amid a thin, relentless wailing. Stefan and Staszek nearly emptied the stock of drugs in the space of two hours, dispensing the carefully hoarded luminal and scopolamine right and left. To the amusement of Rygier, who was guzzling pure alcohol, Stefan took two swigs from the big bottle of bromine. Marglewski was seen heading for the gate lugging two suitcases and a knapsack crammed with his index cards on geniuses. Kauters disappeared into his apartment before midnight. Chaos mounted by the minute. Each ward howled in a different voice, creating a random, polyphonic scream. Stefan passed the dean's room several times in hasty and needless trips up and down the stairs. A sliver of light showed under the door, but there was no sound from within.

It seemed impossible to find a place to hide patients on the hospital grounds. Then Pajączkowski presented the doctors with a fait accompli: he took eleven schizophrenics in remission and three manics into his apartment. He moved a wardrobe in front of the door to conceal them, but it had to be taken away temporarily when the healthiest-looking schizophrenic had a sudden attack. A big chunk of plaster was chipped off when the wardrobe was hurriedly replaced, and Pajączkowski covered the spot with a curtain. Stefan looked in several times. Under other circumstances he would have been amused at the sight of the old man, his mouth full of nails, teetering on a chair supported by Joseph, putting up a curtain rod with a neurological hammer. It was announced that only those with at least two rooms could hide patients. That meant Kauters and Rygier. The latter, now thoroughly drunk, agreed to take a few. Stefan went to the ward to bring out the boy sculptor. He opened the door on a storm of screaming people.

Long strips of bedding whirled around the few remaining light bulbs. Crowing, whistles, and a repetitive hoarse chant of "The Punic War in the Closet!" rose above the general roar. Stefan groped along the wall unnoticed. Twice he was kicked by Paścikowiak, who paced back and forth with long, vigorous strides, as if trying to break free of gravity.

Patients blind with madness spun in demonic pinwheels, threw themselves against walls, and crawled by twos and threes under beds from which their jerking legs stuck out.

Stefan at last reached the boy's room. Once he found him, he had to use his fists to try to clear a path to the door. The boy resisted and dragged Stefan into a corner. There he took a large canvas bundle from under a straw pallet. Only then did he let himself be led out.

When they reached the corridor, Stefan stopped for breath. He was missing several buttons and his nose was bleeding. The wailing behind the doors rose an octave. He handed the boy over to Joseph, who was helping to arrange a hiding place in Marglewski's apartment, and went back downstairs. At the bottom of the stairs he noticed that he was holding something: the bundle the boy had given him. He tucked it under his arm, reached for a cigarette, and was frightened at how his hands shook as he struck a match.

After the third attack among his stowaways, Pajpak gave each of them a dose of luminal. Dawn was breaking as the last of thirty drugged patients were closed into an apartment.

Pajpak, who seemed to be everywhere at once, was personally destroying files, ignoring Stefan's warnings. Wiping his hands after burning papers in a stove, he said, "I'll take the responsibility for this."

Nosilewska, pale but composed, shadowed the director. A fictional post, "chaplain," was created for Father Niezgłoba, who stood in the darkest corner of the pharmacy praying in a piercing whisper.

As he ran aimlessly through the corridor, Stefan bumped into Sekułowski. "Doctor," the poet cried, clutching Stefan's smock, "perhaps I could—why don't you lend me a doctor's coat? After all, you know I'm familiar with psychiatry."

He ran along with Stefan as if they were playing tag. Stefan stopped, gathered his wits, and thought it over. "Why not? It hardly matters at this point. We took care of the priest, so I guess we can do something for you. But . . ."

Sekułowski did not let him finish. They ran to the stairs, shouting back and forth. Pajpak stood on the landing giving the nurses final instructions.

"I say we should just poison them all!" cried Staszek, red as a beet.

"That's not only nonsense, it's criminal," said Pajączkowski. Large drops of sweat ran down his forehead and glistened in his bushy gray eyebrows. "God might change everything at the last minute, and what then?"

"Ignore him," said Rygier contemptuously from the shadows. A bottle peeped out of his pocket.

"You're drunk!"

"Professor," Stefan joined in, Sekułowski shoving him toward the old man, "there's one more thing."

"Well, I don't know," said Pajpak, when he heard Stefan's suggestion. "Why don't you want to come to . . . to my apartment?" He wiped his forehead with a large handkerchief. "All right, of course. Right away. Doctor Nosilewska, you know how to arrange it."

"I'll falsify the records right away," she said in her clear, pleasant voice. "Come with me."

Sekułowski went with her.

"Now, one more thing," said Pajpak. "Someone has to go to see Doctor Kauters. But I can't go alone, it's too awkward."

He waited for Nosilewska to come back from the office. Sekułowski was bustling around the building in Stefan's white coat, and had even appropriated a stethoscope to adorn his pocket. But when he came near enough to the door of the next building to hear the gathering howls, he retreated to the library.

Stefan felt weary. He looked around the corridor, waved his hand, peered through the window to see if it was morning yet, and walked to the pharmacy to take some more bromine. As

187

he was putting the bottle back on the shelf, he heard someone come in.

It was Ładkowski, wearing a loose black suit.

The dean seemed unhappy to find Stefan there. He stood awkwardly in the doorway.

Stefan thought that perhaps Ładkowski was not feeling well. He was pale and seemed not to want to meet Stefan's gaze. He hesitated as if about to leave, even putting his hand on the doorknob, but turned back and came close to Stefan. "Is there any cyanide here?" he asked.

"Excuse me?"

"Is there any potassium cyanide in the pharmacy?"

"Well, yes," mumbled Stefan, unable to collect his thoughts. In his amazement he dropped the bottle of luminal, which shattered on the floor. He bent to pick up the pieces, but then stood and looked expectantly at the dean.

"The key is hanging right there, Excellency. Yes, that one."

The cyanide and other poisons were kept under lock and key in a small cabinet on the wall.

Ładkowski opened a drawer and took out a small glass tube that had contained piramidon. Then he took a jar off the shelf, uncorked it with tongs, and carefully poured white crystals into the tube. He corked it and put it in the upper pocket of his coat. He locked the cabinet, hung the key back on its nail, and turned to go. But he stopped and hung the key back on its nail, and turned to go. But he stopped and said to Stefan, "Please don't tell anyone about this. . . ."

He gripped Stefan's hand, squeezed it with his cold fingers, and said in a half-whisper, "Please."

He hurried out, closing the door softly.

Stefan stood leaning on the table, still feeling Ładkowski's fingers on the back of his hand. He looked around, went back to the cabinet to pour himself some bromine. With the bottle in his hand, he froze.

He had caught a momentary glimpse of Ładkowski's frail old chest through his unbuttoned shirt. It reminded him of a fairy tale about a powerful king, a story that had once obsessed him.

This monarch ruled an enormous kingdom. People for a thousand miles around obeyed him. Once, when he had fallen asleep on his throne in boredom, his courtiers decided to undress him and carry him to the bedchamber. They took off his burgundy coat, under which shined a purple, gold-embroidered mantle. Under that was a silk robe, all stars and suns. Then a bright robe woven with pearls. Then a robe shining with rubies. They removed one robe after another until a great shimmering heap stood beside the throne. They looked around in terror. "Where is our king?" they cried. A wealth of precious robes lay before them, but there was no trace of a living being. The title of the story was "On Majesty, or, Peeling an Onion."

The conference in Kauters's apartment lasted an hour. In the end the surgeon opted for nonintervention: he would know nothing, do nothing. He would admit to familiarity with the operating room alone. Sekułowski would pose as the doctor on his ward. When Nosilewska told Stefan about the discussion, she mentioned that Sister Gonzaga was in Kauters's apartment, sleeping on two armchairs pulled together. Sister Gonzaga? Stefan no longer had the strength to be astonished. He felt numb. He saw everything through a light fog. It was almost six. He saw Rygier in the corridor sitting in a special wheelchair used to transport paralytics. Rygier put the bottle on the floor in front of him and delicately kicked at it, as though delighted by the pure sound of glass.

Stefan was struck by the tension on his face, which seemed to presage an outbreak of tears at any moment. He did not

189

dare say anything, but Rygier suddenly started hiccupping.

"Do you know where Pajączkowski is?" Stefan asked.

"He went out into the garden," said Rygier, hiccupping.

"What for?"

"He's with the priest. They must be praying."

"I see."

Sekułowski emerged from the library and spotted Stefan.

"Where are you going?"

"I'm all in. I think I'll lie down. We'll need our strength in the morning."

Sekułowski seemed heavier in the white coat. The belt was too short to tie until he added a length of bandage.

"I admire, doctor. I couldn't do it."

"Don't be silly. Come to my room."

Stefan noticed a bundle on the radiator in the stairwell. Then he remembered that the boy had given it to him. He picked it up and, curious, unwrapped it. He saw the head of a man wearing a helmet, submerged to the upper lip in a block of stone. The eyes bulged and the cheeks were distended. The invisible mouth, lost in the stone, seemed to scream.

He put the statue on the table in his room, pulled the blanket off the bed, moved the chair, and fell onto his pillow. At that moment, Rygier burst in.

"Listen," he said. "Young Pościk's here. He's taking six patients through the woods to Nieczawy. Do you want to go along, Mr. Sekułowski?"

"Who is it?" Stefan moved his lips voicelessly.

But his whisper was drowned by the poet's questions: "Who? Which patients?"

Stefan raised himself from the bed, fighting sleep.

"Young Pościk, who worked at the substation. He came over from the forest and is waiting downstairs." Rygier was sobering up. "He's taking everyone who didn't get luminal from the old man. Do you want to go or not?"

190

"With the lunatics? Now?" the poet asked, getting out of the chair. His hands were shaking.

"Should I go?" he said, turning to Stefan.

"I can't give you any advice on this."

"After curfew, with the lunatics," Sekułowski calculated half aloud. "No!" he said decisively, but when Rygier reached the doorway, he shouted, "Wait!"

"Make up your mind! He can't wait. It's two hours through the woods!"

"But who is he?"

Sekułowski was plainly asking questions to stall for time. His hand was on the knot of the belt around his coat.

"He's a partisan! He just got here and had an argument with Pajączkowski about the way those patients were doped on luminal."

"Is he reliable?"

"How should I know? Are you coming or not?"

"Is the priest going?"

"No. Well?"

Sekułowski said nothing. Rygier shrugged and left, slamming the door. The poet took a step to follow, then stopped.

"Maybe I should go," he said helplessly.

Stefan's head dropped back on the pillow. He murmured something.

He could hear the poet pacing and talking, but could make no sense of the words. A paralyzing somnolence rose within him.

"Lie down," he said, and fell asleep almost immediately.

A bright light woke him. A rod of some kind was digging into his shoulder. He opened his eyes and lay motionless. He had drawn the blinds the night before and the room was dark. Several tall people were standing at his bed. Groggy with sleep, he shielded his eyes: one of the men was shining a powerful flashlight in his face.

"Wer bist du?" Who are you?

"He's all right. He's a doctor," another voice, somehow familiar, said in German. Stefan gave a start. There were three Germans in dark raincoats, automatics slung over their shoulders. The door to the hall was open. He heard the heavy tread of hobnailed boots outside.

Sekułowski was standing in the corner. Stefan noticed him only when the German shined the light in that direction.

"Is he a doctor too?"

Sekułowski replied in rapid German, his voice breaking. They left one by one. Hutka stood in the door. He left a young soldier in command, ordering him to bring the doctors downstairs. They took the rear staircase. In the pharmacy they saw Pajączkowski, Nosilewska, Rygier, Staszek, the dean, Kauters, and the priest, all guarded by another soldier in a black uniform. The soldier escorting Stefan and the poet entered, closed the door, and took a long look at them. The director stood near the window with his back to the others, his shoulders hunched. Nosilewska sat on a metal stool, Rygier and Staszek in chairs. The day was cloudy but bright, the white of the clouds showing through the rusty leaves. A soldier blocked the door. He was a peasant with a dark, flat face and a crooked jaw. He breathed more and more heavily, and finally shouted in Ukrainian, "Well, doctors, what about you? The Ukraine lives, but you're finished!"

"Please do your duty, as we have done ours, but do not speak to us," said Pajpak in Polish, his voice surprisingly strong. He turned nimbly, drew himself up, and looked at the Ukrainian with his dark eyes.

"You!" murmured the soldier, raising his lumpy fist. The door flung open and hit the soldier in the back.

"What are you doing here?" growled Hutka in German. "Out!" He was wearing his helmet and held his automatic in his left hand, as if about to hit somebody with it.

"Silence!" he shouted, though no one had spoken. "Stay here until you get further orders. No one leaves. I repeat: if we find a single patient hidden, you all pay."

He looked at them with his watery eyes and turned away. Sekułowski called out hoarsely, "Herr . . . Herr Offizier!"

"What now?" snarled Hutka. His dark brown face showed under his helmet. His hand rested on the doorknob.

"Some patients have been hidden in the living quarters."

"What!? What!?"

Hutka rushed toward Sekułowski, grabbed him by the collar, and shook him.

"Where are they, you bastards?"

Sekułowski began to groan and tremble. Hutka called in the duty officer and told him to search all the apartments. The poet, still held by his coat collar, whined rapidly in Polish, "I didn't want all of us to be—" His sleeves were pulled so tightly that he could not move his arms.

"Herr Obersturmführer," shouted Staszek, deathly pale, "he's not a doctor, he's a patient, a mental case!"

Someone sighed. Hutka was stupefied.

"What's that supposed to mean?" the German retorted. "What's the meaning of this, swine of a doctor?"

Staszek, in his poor German, repeated that Sekułowski was a patient.

Niezgłoba slouched toward the window. Hutka looked around at them, beginning to understand. His nostrils flared. "What bastards these swine are, what liars!" he wailed, pressing Sekułowski against the wall. The bottle of bromine on the edge of the table teetered and fell, shattering and splashing its contents over the linoleum.

193

"Well, we will straighten everything out. Let me see your papers!"

A Ukrainian—apparently a senior aide, because he wore two silver stripes on his epaulets—was called in from the hall to help translate the papers. Everyone except Nosilewska had them. A guard accompanied her upstairs while Hutka stood before Kauters, examining his papers at great length and seeming to calm down.

"Ah," said the German. "Volksdeutsch, are you? Excellent. Why did you get mixed up in this Polish swindle?"

Kauters explained that he had known nothing about it. He spoke harsh but correct German.

Nosilewska came back with her Medical Association identity card. Hutka waved her away and turned to Sekułowski, who was still standing by the cabinet against the wall.

"Komm."

"Herr Offizier . . . I'm not ill. I'm thoroughly well."

"Are you a doctor?"

"Yes—I mean, no, but I really can't—I'll . . ."

"Komm."

Hutka was now completely calm—too calm. He stood still, nearly smiling, his raincoat rustling with every movement. He signaled with his index finger, as one would to a child: "Komm."

Sekułowski took a step and fell to his knees.

"Mercy! Please! I want to live. I'm not insane."

"Enough!" Hutka roared. "Traitor! You betrayed your poor, crazy brothers."

Two shots rang out behind the building. The windowpanes rattled and the instruments on the shelves trembled.

Sekułowski, wrapped in the folds of his doctor's coat, fell at the German's boots.

"Franke!" Hutka called out.

Another German came in and jerked Sekułowski by the shoulders so powerfully that the poet, tall and fat though he was, snapped upright like a rag doll.

"My mother was German!" he squealed in a falsetto as he was dragged to the door. He grabbed frantically for a hand-hold, squirming and gripping the doorframe but not daring to defend himself against the blows. Franke raised his rifle butt and methodically smashed Sekułowski's fingers.

"Have mercy!" howled Sekułowski in German, and then "Mother of God!" in Polish. Fat tears rolled down his face.

The German lost his temper. Sekułowski now had hold of the doorknob. Franke took him around the waist, leaned into him, tensed, and pushed with all his might. They flew into the corridor, Sekułowski falling to the stone floor with a thud. The German reached back to close the door, giving the doctors a last glance at his flushed, sweaty face.

"Disgusting!" he said and slammed the door.

A large clump of bushes blocked the pharmacy window. Further on, beyond scattered trees, a blank wall rose. The cries of patients and the rasping voices of the Germans were distinct, though muffled. The crack of rifle shots seemed louder, somehow solidified. First there was a thick volley, then a sound like soft bags falling. Then silence.

A strident voice called in German: "Twenty more!"

Shots trilled off the wall. Sharp, melancholy whistles marked the occasional ricochet. At one point an automatic rifle barked, but generally it was small arms. Another silence was followed by the scraping of many feet and the now monotonous cry: "Twenty more!"

Two or three pistol shots, high-pitched and terse, sounded like corks coming out of bottles.

One inhuman penetrating scream rang out. There was a sound of crying from above, as if coming from the second floor. It went on for a long time.

The doctors sat motionless, their eyes glued to the nearest objects. Stefan felt stuporous. At first he had tried to cling to something: perhaps Hutka, who made the decisions, might somehow . . . there was life even in death . . . but a German shout interrupted his last reflection. There was a crashing of broken branches, red leaves fluttered outside the window, and breathy sobbing and the sound of boots on gravel were heard quite close by.

A shot rang out like thunder. A scream rose and collapsed.

Fast-moving clouds, their shapes changing constantly, filled the fragment of visible sky. The shooting stopped after ten. A strange sense of torpor set in. A quarter of an hour later the automatic rifles chattered again, the ensuing silence filled with the howling of the sick and the raucous voices of the Germans.

At noon the doctors heard heavy footsteps moving around the building; a dog barked and a woman squealed briefly. The door suddenly opened and the Ukrainian soldier came in.

"Everyone out! Fast!" he shouted in Ukrainian from the doorway. A German helmet appeared behind him.

"Everyone out!" he repeated, shouting at the top of his lungs. Dust and sweat were mixed on his face; his eyes looked drunken, trembling.

The doctors filed out. Stefan found himself next to Nosilewska. The corridor was empty except for a heap of crumpled bedding right outside the door. Long black streaks on the floor led to the stairs. A great mass lay propped against the radiator at the bend in the corridor: a corpse bent double, a black icicle protruding from its smashed skull. A gnarled yellow heel stuck out from under the cherry-colored robe. Everybody stepped over it except the German bringing up the rear, who kicked

196

the foot with his boot. The shapes walking ahead of Stefan danced before his eyes. He took hold of Nosilewska's shoulder. He was still holding on when they reached the library.

Piles of books had been thrown to the floor from the two bookcases nearest the door. The pages fluttered as the doctors stepped over them on the way in. Two Germans waiting by the door entered last. They sat down on the comfortable sofa, upholstered in red plush.

Everything seemed to waver in Stefan's eyes. The room throbbed and turned gray, then collapsed like a burst blister. He fainted for the first time in his life.

When he came to, he realized that he was lying on something warm. His head rested on Nosilewska's knees; Pajpak was holding his legs up.

"What happened to the nurses?" Stefan asked distractedly.

"They were all sent to Bierzyniec this morning."

"What about us?"

No one answered. Stefan stood up, staggered, but felt that he would not faint again. Steps approached from outside; a soldier came in.

"Ist der Professor Lonkoski hier?" he asked.

There was silence. At last Rygier whispered, "Dean. Your Excellency."

The dean, slumped in his chair when he heard the German's call, slowly straightened. His large, heavy, expressionless eyes moved slowly from face to face. He grasped the arms of the chair, raised himself up with an effort, and reached into the upper pocket of his coat. He felt for something with a movement of his flattened hand. The priest, in his black cassock, stepped toward him, but the dean gestured categorically and walked to the door.

"Kommen Sie, bitte," said the German, and graciously allowed him to go first.

The rest sat in silence until two shots roared thunderously in a closed space very nearby. Even the Germans, talking as they sat on the couch, fell silent. Kauters, bathed in sweat, stretched his Egyptian profile into a notched line and wrung his hands until his joints cracked. Rygier twisted his mouth childishly and bit his lip. Only Nosilewska—bent forward, elbows on her knees, her chin resting on her fists—seemed calm. Calm and beautiful.

Stefan felt something swelling in his stomach, his whole body seemed enormous and slick with sweat, a hideous trembling crept over his skin, but he thought that Nosilewska would be beautiful even in death, and he took a perverse satisfaction in the thought.

"It seems that . . . that we, too . . ." Rygier whispered to Staszek.

All of them sat on the red chairs except the priest, who stood between two bookcases in the darkest corner. Stefan rushed over to him.

The priest was whispering.

"They're killing . . ." said Stefan.

"Pater noster, qui est in coelis," whispered the priest.

"Father, it's not true!"

"Sanctificetur nomen Tuum."

"You're wrong, Father, it's a lie," Stefan whispered. "There's nothing there, nothing! I understood it when I fainted. This room, and us, everything, it's only our blood. When that stops flowing and the heart stops beating, even heaven dies! Do you hear me, Father?"

Stefan pulled at his cassock.

"Fiat voluntas Tua," whispered the priest.

"There's nothing, no color, no smell, not even darkness. . . ."

"It is this world that does not exist," the priest said quietly, his ugly, pained face looking back at Stefan.

The Germans burst out laughing. Kauters suddenly stood up and went over to them. "Excuse me," he said in German, "but Herr Obersturmführer took my papers away. Would you happen to know whether . . . ?"

"Be patient," answered a stout, wide-shouldered German with red-veined cheeks. He turned back to his comrade and spoke. "You know, the houses were already on fire and I thought everyone inside was dead. All of a sudden this woman comes running out through the flames, heading right for the woods. She's running like a madwoman, holding onto a goose. Unbelievable! Fritz wanted to take her out, but he was laughing so hard he couldn't shoot straight."

They both laughed. Kauters stood motionless in front of them, then suddenly his face twisted up strangely and he forced out a reedy "ha ha ha!"

The storyteller's expression darkened.

"What are you laughing at, doctor?" he asked. "There's nothing for you to laugh at."

White spots appeared on Kauters's cheeks.

"I . . . " he croaked. "I am German!"

The German looked up at him carefully.

"Are you now? Well in that case go ahead and laugh."

Footsteps sounded in the hallway, powerful and hard, instantly recognizable as German.

"Father, do you believe?" Stefan asked with his last ounce of strength.

"I believe."

A tall officer they had not seen before came in. His uniform fit as if it had been painted on, and a dull sparkle showed on his epaulets. His bare head was long, with a noble forehead and chestnut hair speckled with gray. Light flashed in his steel-rimmed glasses when he looked at them. The surgeon approached him, tensed, and held out his hand.

"Von Kauters."

"Thiessdorff."

"Herr Doktor, what has happened to our dean?" Kauters asked.

"Don't worry about him. I'll take him to Bieschinetz in my car. He's packing his things now."

"Really?" Kauters exclaimed.

The German blushed and shook his head. "Mein Herr!" Then he smiled and said abruptly, "You must believe what I say."

"Why are we being held here?"

"Come now. You were in real trouble before, but Hutka has calmed down now. You're under guard so our Ukrainians can't do you any harm. They go for blood like hounds, you know."

"Really?" asked Kauters, amazed.

"Oh yes, they're like falcons: you have to feed them raw meat," the German psychiatrist said with a laugh.

The priest came over and spoke in broken German. "Herr Doktor, how has this come about? Man and doctor and patient, the people who have been shot. Death!"

At first it seemed the German would turn away or raise a hand to shield himself from this black-clad interference, but he suddenly brightened.

"Every nation," he answered, his voice deep, "is like an organism. Sometimes the body's sick cells have to be excised. This was such an excision."

He looked over the priest's shoulder at Nosilewska. His nostrils flared.

"Aber Gott, Gott," the priest repeated.

Nosilewska sat silent and motionless, and the German spoke more loudly as he looked at her. "Let me explain it to you another way. In the days of Caesar Augustus there was a Roman viceroy in Galilee who reigned over the Jews. His name was Pontius Pilate. . . ."

The German's eyes were burning.

"Stefan," Nosilewska said in Polish, "please tell him to let me go. I don't need anyone's protection and I can't stay here any longer, because . . ." She broke off.

Stefan, deeply moved—it was the first time she had called him by his first name—went over to Thiessdorff. The German bowed politely.

Stefan asked if they could leave.

"Do you want to leave? All of you?"

"Frau Doktor Nosilewska," said Stefan, rather helplessly.

"Oh, yes. Yes, of course. Once again, you must be patient."

The German kept his word. They were released at dusk. The building was silent, dark, and empty. Stefan went to his room to pack a few things. When he turned on the light, he saw Sekułowski's notebook on the table and threw it into his open suitcase. Then he saw the sculpture next to it. He felt sick when he realized that its creator was somewhere quite near, buried under dozens of bodies in the grave that had been dug that morning.

For a moment he fought the pain tearing at his stomach, then fell on the bed and sobbed briefly, without tears. Then he was calm. He quickly took what he needed, knelt on his suitcase to close it, and locked it. Someone came in. Nosilewska. She carried a briefcase. She handed Stefan a long, white object: a sheaf of papers.

"I found this in the hallway," she said. When she saw that Stefan did not understand, she added, "Sekułowski lost it. I thought that since you took care of him . . . It's—it was his."

Stefan stood with his arms at his sides.

"Was?" he said. "Yes, it was."

"It's better not to think about it now. Don't," said Nosi-

201

lewska, in a physician's tone. He picked up his suitcase, took the papers, hesitated, and finally slid them into his pocket.

"We're going, aren't we?" she asked. "Rygier and Pajączkowski are staying overnight. Your friend is with them. They're leaving in the morning. The Germans promised to take their things to the train."

"What about Kauters?" asked Stefan without looking up.

"Von Kauters, you mean?" Nosilewska replied slowly. "I don't know. Maybe he'll stay here."

When he looked at her, puzzled, she added, "This is going to be an SS hospital. I heard him talking about it with Thiessdorff."

"Ah, yes," said Stefan. His head was starting to hurt, from temples to forehead.

"Do you want to stay? Because I'm going."

"I admire your composure."

"There's not much left. It's just about used up. I have to leave. I have to get out of here," she repeated.

"I'll come with you," he said suddenly, feeling that he too would be unable to touch equipment still warm from the touch of those now dead, or to inhale air in which their breath seemed still to hang.

"Let's go through the woods," she said. "It's shorter. And Hutka told me the Ukrainians are patrolling the roads. I'd rather not run into them."

When they reached the ground floor, Stefan hesitated. "What about the others?"

She understood what he meant. "It might be easier for us, and for them too. All of us need different people now, different surroundings."

They walked toward the gate: above them dark trees soughed like the surface of a cold sea. There was no moon. A large dark shape suddenly loomed in front of them.

"Who goes there?" a voice asked in German.

The white beam of a flashlight fell on them. In the reflection from the leaves they recognized Hutka. He was patrolling the yard.

"Go," he said, waving them on.

They passed him in silence.

"Hey!" he called.

They stopped.

"Your first and only obligation now is to keep silent. Understand?" His voice held a threat. Maybe it was because of the glaring, shadow-sliced light, but he seemed somehow tragic walking in the long coat that fell to his boots, a seam of teeth showing in his face.

Much later, Stefan spoke: "How can they do such things and live?"

They were on the damp road, past the stone arch with the faded inscription black against the sky, when light shined around them again. Hutka was waving farewell with wide swings of the flashlight. Then all was blackness.

They veered off the road at the second bend and slogged laboriously through the mud, heading for the forest. Trees, ever denser and taller, surrounded them. Their feet sank into dry leaves that babbled like water at a ford. They walked for a long time.

Stefan looked at his watch. By then they should have been at the edge of the woods, from which they would be able to see the railroad station. But he said nothing. They walked on and on, bumping into each other; the suitcase felt heavier. The forest sighed steadily. Through the branches they caught rare glimpses of a ghostly night cloud. They stopped and spoke in front of a great spreading sycamore.

"We've lost our way."

"So it seems."

203

"We should have taken the road."

They tried in vain to figure out where they were. It had gotten darker.

Clouds covered the sky, forming a low backdrop to the leafless branches that stirred in the wind. The breeze rattled the twigs. Then rain began to fall, and dripped down their faces.

When they stopped to rest, they noticed a squat shape nearby: some sort of barn or cottage. The trees thinned out and they walked into an open space.

"This is Wietrzniki," Stefan said slowly. "We're nine kilometers from the road, eleven from town."

They had walked in a broad arc in the wrong direction.

"We'll never get to the train in time. Unless we find horses."

Stefan did not answer: it seemed impossible. The people were long gone. A few days ago the Germans had burned the neighboring village to the ground, and everyone had fled.

They climbed over a low fence and tapped at the windows and door. Dead silence. A dog barked, then another, and finally waves of steady barking rang through the area. An isolated cottage stood on a little hill above the village. A glow appeared in one of the windows.

Stefan hammered on the door until he shook. He was about to lose hope when it opened to reveal a tall, rumpled peasant, the whites of his eyes shining in his dark face. A white unbuttoned shirt peeked out under the jacket he had thrown on.

"We're . . . we're doctors from the hospital in Bierzyniec, and we're lost. We need a place to sleep, please," Stefan began, sensing that he was saying the wrong thing. But anything he said would be wrong. He knew peasants.

The man stood immobile, blocking the entrance.

"All we're asking for is a place to sleep," Nosilewska said, quiet as a distant echo.

The peasant did not move.

"We'll pay," Stefan tried.

The peasant still did not speak. He stood there. Stefan took his wallet out of an inside pocket.

"I don't need your money," the peasant said suddenly. "What people like you need is a bullet."

"What do you mean? The Germans let us leave. We got lost, we were trying to make the train."

"They shoot, burn, beat," the peasant continued in a monotone, stepping out across the threshold. He pulled the door shut behind him and stood, tall, in the open. The rain was coming down harder.

"What can you do?" he said finally, shrugging.

He walked away from the house. Stefan and Nosilewska followed. There was a thatched shed in the yard. The man turned the simple latch on the door. The inside smelled of old hay and aromatic dust that tickled the nose.

"Here," said the peasant. He paused for a moment and added, "You can sleep on the hay. But don't crush the bundles."

"Thank you very much," said Stefan. "Will you take something after all?"

He tried to press a banknote into the peasant's hand.

"That won't stop a bullet," the peasant said dryly. "What can you do?" he said again, more quietly.

"Thank you," Stefan repeated helplessly.

The peasant stood there for another moment, then said, "Good night." He left, turning the latch.

Stefan was standing just inside the door. He stretched out a hand like a blind man: he always had trouble finding his way in darkness. Nosilewska shuffled about on the straw. He took off the cold, heavy jacket that had stuck to his back; water dripped off it. He would have liked to have taken off his trousers too. He bumped into some sort of pole and almost fell over, but steadied himself on his suitcase. Then he remembered that he had a flashlight inside. He pawed at the lock. Along with the flashlight he found a piece of chocolate. Setting the light on the ground, he looked in his pockets for Sekułowski's papers. Nosilewska scattered straw on the dirt floor and covered it with a blanket. Stefan sat down on the blanket's edge and unrolled the sheets of paper. The first one contained several words. The handwriting fluttered between the ruled lines as if caught in a net. At the top was Sekułowski's name, and below it the title: "My World." Stefan turned the sheet over. It was blank. So was the next one. White and empty every one.

"Nothing," he said. "There's nothing."

A fear so powerful came over him that he sought Nosilewska's gaze. She sat bent over, the plaid blanket draped over her. From under it she tossed out her blouse, skirt, and underwear, all heavy with moisture.

"Empty," Stefan repeated. He wanted to say something, but it came out a hoarse groan.

"Come here."

He looked at her. Her hands brushed back the dark waves of her hair.

"I can't," he whispered. "I can't think. That boy. But Sekułowski . . . It was Staszek who . . ."

"Come here," she repeated, gently, almost sleepily. He looked at her in wonder. Extending her arms from under the blanket, she stroked him like a child. He leaned against her.

"I'm bankrupt," he said. "Like my father."

She held him and stroked his head.

"Don't think about it," she whispered. "Don't think about anything."

He felt her breasts and her hands against his face. The only

206

light came from the flicker of the fading flashlight, which had rolled into the hay. Shadows laced its feeble illumination. He could hear the slow, peaceful rhythm of her heart, which spoke to him in the old language, the language he understood best. He was still wondering at that when softly, without breathing, she kissed him on the mouth.

Darkness covered them. Hay crunched under the fuzzy blanket and the woman gave him pleasure, but not in the usual way. At every instant she controlled herself and she controlled him. Later, exhausted, holding her beautiful body without a trace of passion but with all the force of despair, he cried on her breast. When he calmed down, he saw that she was lying on her back, slightly above him, and her face, too, was so calm in the last light. He dared not ask if she loved him. To offer yourself was like giving a stranger your last bit of food: it was more than love. It suddenly occurred to him that he knew nothing about her; he could not even remember her first name.

"Listen," he whispered quietly.

But she put her hand over his mouth, gently yet decisively. She picked up the edge of the blanket and wiped away his tears, kissing him lightly on the cheek.

Then even his curiosity faded, and in the arms of this unfamiliar woman he became, for an instant, as empty and blank as at the moment of his birth.

Kraków, September 1948

207

LEM
    Lem, Stanislaw.
    Hospital of the
Transfiguration

PLEASE DO NOT REMOVE CARD FROM POCKET

By returning material on date due, you will help save
the cost of postage for overdue notices.
We hope you enjoy the library. Come again and bring
your friends!

FALMOUTH PUBLIC LIBRARY
Falmouth, Mass. 02540
548-0280

DEMCO